SKELETON LAKE

TENTH ANNIVERSARY EDITION

ANGELA KULIG

ONE

My mouth was no longer the worst of it. Dryness tore at my cracked lips with every jagged breath I forced out. That feeling seemed to travel from the ends of my dark, tangled hair to the tips of my bare feet. I ran without direction, without a goal.

I liked the feeling of the escape. I liked pretending I could.

Deep footprints and tiny droplets of red ruined the winter landscape behind me as I darted past the tree line. Terrible blotches that looked black in the moonless night were all that remained of my hands. I had unconsciously torn away at the flesh with my own fingernails.'

My heart continued to beat even though I knew it had already given up. Broken, but not silenced, it seemed determined to win a race against the pounding of my steps.

That was when I saw it glowing with the reflection of a million different universes. Tendrils of steam rose from all the edges and danced across the top of the lake. I couldn't remember seeing anything like it before.

Later, I would learn it was Skeleton Lake, but at the time, it only looked like my salvation.

What would it be like to drown? Did it hurt? How would it feel floating there, weightless, until my very life drained away?

I sprinted down a decaying wooden dock without looking back. Boards creaked below my weight. Pieces splintered off and landed in the water with a plink that sounded like hailstones.

I remember the sounds. I remember the smell of the old gray timber being torn from rusted nails.

I still can't remember the splash.

Drowning was nothing like I thought it would be. To start, it was slow. Time seemed to stretch out forever. The water was warm and pleasant after running through the snow. My wounds felt soothed by the murky waters. Even as liquid swirled into my ears, I could imagine I was at home in a bath instead of floating toward my oblivion.

I never closed my eyes. My vision blurred then somehow refocused on two places at once. Part of me stared at the late eighties wall paper in the bathroom, which my father stubbornly refused to update. The other part of me was completely aware of the lake, and the sky above me.

The stars were nearly invisible. Blackness stretched over my head like an old sheet, letting in just a little light through its worn places.

There was still more darkness below, where the muddy bottom waited to welcome me permanently into its grasp.

Even though I floated, I felt weighted down with so many things—Mom and Dad alone in the old farmhouse, unaware anything was wrong, all the friends I had until tonight, and the crushing weight of other people's secrets.

Then there was light. Not a warm white light like everyone talks about, but a ghostly blue one. I wondered what its presence meant for my afterlife, if there was such a thing.

That was my last thought before the panic set in. Until I started burning.

Everything until that point had seemed so surreal. Had I ever stopped to think? There had only been the need to escape.

The blue light was right on top of me. I could tell it was close enough to reach out and grab me, but I was still surprised when it did. It seared my burning skin with ice cold fingers like instant frostbite on sunburned flesh—a cold and brittle feeling that belonged to a moving skeleton. Was it Death? Did such a specter really exist?

I let out the last of the air from my lungs as the black bled in from the edges of my vision. It filled everything. And then my stomach took a big flop. My whole body felt stuck in a Marlow shaped elevator shaft, and

I had come to a sudden halt before being jolted upwards.

Then there was nothing.

I was unaware if I would ever leave the lake, unaware if it mattered at all.

Two

I could hear my eyelids separating, and I didn't understand why they protested. When I blinked the crust out of my eyes there was a white blur above me. It was so blindingly bright I wanted to look away from it, but my neck ached and wouldn't budge. This might be that light that people talk about it, but my head was still filled with a ghastly blue one—one that seemed to laugh at me from every direction at once.

When the image above me came into sharper focus, I realized it was nothing more than a yellowing ceiling fan. Two of its decorative bulbs were burned out. I couldn't see what was directly behind me and the rest of the room was sloppily painted black—or maybe a deep, deep blue.

This wasn't my grandparents' old farmhouse, but where was it and how did I get here? The dark walls seemed to nag at my cloudy head. The blackness seemed oddly wrong, but still familiar. As far as I could remember, I had never been in this room.

Visions of the blue light returned, along with images of the water I felt sure I should have drowned in. Only I couldn't have. I still seemed to be alive, and in pain at that. So unless Hell had undergone a recent remodeling to resemble a Goth kid's bedroom, I must not be dead, yet the thought made my neck throb.

Pieces from the rest of the evening slowly drifted back to me. Each part of the puzzle stung a bit more than the last. I had snuck out of the house. There was no way my parents would have let me leave dressed like I had been—or otherwise. At the time, I felt it was something I had to do; now I just wished I had never left home.

Because he wasn't worth it.

There was a party at Rachelle's house

that I could not have cared less about, but I knew Tyson would be there. Tyson King, last time I checked, was still supposed to be my boyfriend. Things had been tense since Thanksgiving, and saying I did not expect to see him there with his arm snaked around a willing Rachelle was an understatement.

I knew the moment I entered the house something was wrong. As I checked my reflection in the hallway mirror, smoothing out the green dress Tyson loved, people whispered and stared. I ignored them, just as I had been doing for months. I wandered into the crowded living room, and that's where I found them, alone on the loveseat against a window. I could see the snow falling into the yard, but my eyes were locked onto Tyson's face, waiting for him to see me.

When he looked up, there was nothing. No shock, no remorse, no guilt. Maybe there had never been anything there at all. I spun around and fell, one of my spiky heels had lodged itself in a knot on the floor, and then he was there.

I hated myself for what I wanted him to say. I wanted him to smile, lie, and let everything go back to the way it had been when I was blissfully unaware. He just took my hands in his, pulled me close, and said it wasn't worth pretending anymore. *I wasn't worth it.*

So I ran. The cold wind chapped my whole body as I clawed at my hands in a fruitless attempt to get him off my skin. I had walked the half mile to Rachelle's house from my newly inherited farm, but my coat, gloves, and common sense were still sitting in Rachelle Wood's entryway; and I was flying in the wrong direction.

First I went over a fence and through a snow covered field, then the woods. The air was drying me out, my heart was already withered. Then, oddly, I felt as if someone was behind me, watching me, but it could be no more than the wind so I shook the feeling away.

Why had Tyson affected me so? I had no idea. Right now I was lost physically, not just emotionally. Without causing more neck pain, I pulled my hands above the old quilt I was tucked into. I still did not look down because I was sure they were completely mangled. Instead, I wiggled my fingers. I could feel the cotton fabric beneath the tips, but the movement did not hurt.

So I made myself look, but my hands were completely unharmed. No blood, no torn flesh, and no bones. They were exactly how they had been in Math class Friday, when my mind kept straying from the Calculus I could never get my head around. I had been twirling my purple pencil round and round, thinking I should file my nails.

If the whole thing had really been a nightmare, how did I end up here? Footsteps clomped and shuffled outside the dark room, several sets. Though they did not seem to whisper, nothing they said seemed to make sense through the wooden door. I closed my eyes tight just before it swung open.

"She's still asleep," said a girl's voice. "We don't even know if she can live through this. She's too old. I think you should have done the humane thing and left her in the lake."

I did my best to not tense beneath the sheets as two males laughed at the foot of my bed. Freaking out would make it obvious I wasn't really asleep.

"I'd say you were jealous, Lena," chuckled a familiar boy's voice. "Besides, she's not for me, she's for—"

"Stop it, Alex," said another boy's voice, and I was sure I knew this one.

I'm not for anyone! I wanted to scream, but I didn't dare. I needed them to leave and maybe then I could sneak out the window. I was getting pretty good at that.

"She's lasted this long. I think if it was going to kill her it wouldn't have saved her to begin with."

Was he talking about that blue light I remember? I didn't understand what they meant at all, and I really did not want to stick around and find out. I heard the girl sigh. It was more of a squeak and, in the blankness behind my eyes, my imagination couldn't draw a vision of that noise coming from either of the boys in this room.

"Fine," said Alex. "Enjoy your corpse. Lena and I are going to go have some more animated fun."

Enjoy?

Only two pairs of steps left the room, and I wondered if I could fight off the one boy if he decided to try and enjoy me a bit too much. Silently, he sat down on the end of the bed. He didn't make a move, I couldn't even hear him breathe but I thought I could feel his eyes on my face. I worked hard at convincing myself it was all in my head.

He coughed. Not a real sick cough, but as though he was clearing his throat or trying to get my attention.

"I know you're awake, Marlow." I did not move. If I didn't move, he would know nothing. "I can tell by the way your eyelids twitch whenever someone said anything you didn't like."

Well, he had me there. Now I just wasn't opening my eyes to give him the satisfaction of being right, because that would be just like Raiden Mast.

He and his cocky grin appeared in full color in my head, making it throb with every *thunk thunk* of my heart. He made me every bit as uneasy in my imagination as he did in real life. Only if I was being completely honest with myself, the creeps he usually gave me when I spied him across the courtyard at school seemed to have vanished.

Maybe it was the close distance. I hadn't been within ten feet of him since ninth grade history—or maybe my body was just too tired to conjure that typical knee jerk, goose bump inducing reaction. Or maybe something was really wrong with me.

I opened my eyes. I planned to thank him for his hospitality and to demand he take me home, *right now*. But when I looked up, intending to glare at him, I was struck by the blue of his eyes. It was a familiar color, though I couldn't remember ever having paid them much attention before. I don't even think I had known they were blue.

My words jammed in my throat. This wasn't the creeps at all.

"Marlow, there is something I should tell you."

He looked away. I wanted to grab his attention, I wanted to make him look at me again and never stop. He seemed to be staring at a blank spot on the wall; there was a dent there just above the floorboard, like someone had kicked it.

"Is this your room?"

His eyes shot back to mine.

"Yes," he breathed.

"Did you bring me here?" I asked, pleading for his gaze to stay focused on mine.

"Yes," he repeated again.

"Why?"

His eyes shot back to the dent in the wall, and at first I thought he wouldn't answer me.

"Marlow, I hate to tell you this but last night—"

Last night I what? I thought. "Nearly drowned? Got made a fool of in front of a room full of people? What?"

"Last night you... died."

THREE

"Oh," tumbled from my lips like rocks, before settling in my stomach.

"Oh," was all I could say.

Is there even a coherent response to something so impossible? At this moment I should have been hurling myself through the window. The sound of breaking glass as we sailed through the air together should have been my only goodbye. *I should be running away*. That is, after all, what I do.

I just sat there lips puckered up like they would have been when I was a child pretending to be a little fish. I guess vowel sounds make me look stupid, but they seemed to make Raiden completely insane.

"Oh!" he said incredulously, shoulders shaking like he couldn't decide whether to laugh, or punch another hole in his wall. Since I was sitting there, I felt as though I should be contemplating the inconceivable—that he was telling the truth. But I had thought enough about death the previous night to last a lifetime. Absently, I wondered what had triggered the first dent in the drywall.

"Oh!" he said again. This time he spoke more to the heavens, or the thickly painted black ceiling, than me or anyone else. Especially me it seemed. "Are you mental?" he spat at me, rage forming behind those blue eyes. The fierce intensity left me with no doubt they could do more to bruise me than either of his fists.

My tongue felt heavy in my mouth. "What should I say?" I asked, and something shot through his gaze for a moment. So quick, I had already begun chalking it up to my imagination. His lips moved, not to answer, but to ask me more questions I didn't want to hear.

"Let's try something else," he said, tension still radiating across his shoulder blades. "What were you doing last night?"

"Other than dying?" I asked, surprised that I so easily formed the word *dying*. Surprised it didn't cut.

"Other than dying," he repeated.

He would ask me the one thing I didn't want to explain, couldn't explain. Not without delving into things I had no intention of sharing with him or anyone else. Even if I knew he would hear about it come Monday morning, I'd rather put off any further mortification for as long as possible. He seemed to sense my unease at the question, and in a kinder voice he asked, "What were you doing at the lake?"

My head did not want to work as it usually would. It felt slow, like a computer without enough memory to process such a complex question. So few words to ask so many questions I didn't want to answer. What was I doing alone, in the middle of nowhere, in the snow? The better question would be, *why there*? But I didn't know the answer to that question either, and it wasn't the question that would trip him up, and save whatever pride I could salvage from the incident with my former friends. The right question slid from my mouth without much thought.

"Why were you at the lake, Raiden?"

And it did register, that perhaps that sounded exceptionally ungrateful, but he didn't seem to take offense. In fact, he seemed almost deliriously amused. The "ah ha" I had been waiting to shout died in my throat as his grin grew. His eyes crinkled, and his face looked like it might split from the pressure of keeping some snide remark inside. I wanted to demand to know what was so hilarious.

I didn't though, because I was positive it would cause me even worse embarrassment. I said nothing, and he just stood there, face screwed up like he had eaten something sour and liked it.

Finally, he unfurled his arms that had been knotted across his chest. His face still plastered in sheer glee. He strolled past the bed and to the window, my only visible means of escape, and threw open the curtains. At first, I was struck by the inconceivable notion that maybe Raiden could read my mind. That maybe he was offering me this avenue of departure as he gestured casually to the large squares of glass, but we were on the second floor.

Outside it was still dark. On the edge of the sky, the stream of stars gave way to a lightness that would soon grow into the sun. I gazed at the sky as it turned scarlet and plum for far too long. I kept my eyes locked there to avoid looking below it, where I was sure the spectacle of the sky would be repeated in the glassy top of the lake—the one that I'd drowned in last night.

Later, when I could again think clearly, I couldn't exactly recall how I had known the lake was there beneath the window, and below the beautiful sky. However, I can tell you now that even then, returning to the lake would always feel like returning home—long before I knew why.

"It's beautiful," he said, sliding past me again.

That was the exact moment I noticed his

scent. Musky, like the forest had been right before the lake. It was nice, I wondered how I hadn't noticed it before because it was everywhere in the room, in the sheets, and penetrating my skin as I slept in his bed.

"The lake?" I asked him.

Assuming that was what he had meant, but he said, "The sky," with a deep breath and a sigh. "The lake is nothing but a false idol. Tormenting me like a cruel god. Reminding me for all my days, and every last dream filled night, that what it gives to us it can so easily take away."

He was looking at the sky again, but his speech had ruined the beauty of the moment, and again I was curious. He spoke of the lake as if it were a person, something alive, or in his words, a god. *What can a lake give?* I wondered. None of it made sense, but it seemed like he was talking about me.

"Are you—" I started, thinking that perhaps that line of thought was a bit vain. Unfortunately, it was the only line of thought I had. His words seemed to have reopened wounds that had seeped a profound sadness into the room, and I couldn't bear to be the one who caused it. "The lake spared my life," I said, wondering if it had played an even bigger role in my survival than Raiden pulling me out of it did.

"It killed you," he shot back.

"It didn't ask me to throw myself into it."

He looked at me again. The amused expression that had been wiped from his face a moment before returned faster than I could blink.

"Didn't it?" he asked, sarcasm dripping from his smile. His hands moved to tighten around the bed post.

Unintentionally, I bit down on my tongue. Blood immediately begun pooling in my molars, and I did my best to swallow down the coppery taste. Again, he asked me what I was doing at the lake, gently this time—a change in tactics—like he was starting to realize if he pushed me too hard, I might break. I still didn't want to tell him, but I could tell my resolve was wearing thin. The circumstances that had led me to the lake sounded cowardly and irrational even in my head, but tonight, so did everything. It was as if some Siren, or demon from

Hell, had called my name and led me to this fate.

Only nothing was as impossible as what he told me next. At first, he said nothing. He just listened as I told him about Tyson. About how that had hurt more than I ever knew it could. I was embarrassed. Once I started talking, it felt so good I didn't want to stop. Like a cracked dam on a river, bursting free with an alarming speed. I wasn't even sure if he could catch everything I was saying. He didn't speak at all, just nodded occasionally and frowned.

When I was done, I felt out of breath, and less burdened than when I had started.

"You might not believe this now," he said, "but you are better off without that apparition."

"He is pretty foul," I agreed.

"You have no idea what kind of specter he is. I am sure you will, on Monday."

I shivered. I didn't want to think about Monday, but something told me he wasn't just talking about the rumor mill.

"Enough about him," he said.

"None of that tells me how you ended up in my backyard."

I shrugged, and the quilt fell below my waist. "I was running away."

His eyes narrowed. I could tell he was processing what kind of path I would have taken to end up where I did. He may have even seen my trail in the snow.

"The thing is..." he started.

Pausing for the first time since I had woken, as if wondering what to say next.

"Most people, Marlow... *all* people go out of their way to avoid Skeleton Lake. In fact, if you took the entire population of our school and stood them a foot from its banks, the only souls to see it would be the ones in this house."

"I don't understand." I really, really didn't. The lake was real, very real, but it was also different. It had been strange. Hot in the middle of winter with snow on the ground. Tendrils of steam had stretched off of it like the arms of spirits. "It's real."

"It is," he said.

"I saw it," and I'd felt that it had had *seen* me.

"I know, but everyone else? They don't."

It was an eerie, I impossible idea. How could we see it when everyone else couldn't? My pulse raced and my mind went right along with it.

"If they looked at the lake, they would see just a field, and then they would be struck by a very real sense of dread. They would need to go home and count their loved ones and watch the news for the disaster they would believe to be looming, and they would never know why."

"Why?" I asked.

"Skeleton Lake, like everything else in this world that is unnatural—that is, *magic*—has survived this long by hiding itself from humans."

I couldn't decide which word made me wearier. *Magic,* like it really existed, or *humans*, like he wasn't one, and again Raiden spoke of the lake like it was alive.

"Are there monsters?" I asked, amazed my voice didn't shake as my insides did at the question.

"Tons."

"In the lake?"

"Depends on your definition of monster." The corners of his mouth twitched up, a brief nod to his grin from earlier.

"There was a blue light..."

"Um," he stuttered. "I'm afraid, that was me."

Like so many times since I woke up here, I thought he had to be joking. I remembered a supernatural blue glow as it moved towards me in the black, black water. I remember floating there, as I waited to die, feeling like I was being laughed at in surround sound. Then I remembered Raiden's obnoxious smirk. I could feel my eyes closing into slits. Impossible, but true?

"Are you a ghost?" I asked. *Am I?*

"No."

I wasn't sure that was any more comforting. Did that bring us back to insane then?

"I'm a skeleton," he said.

"And now, so are you."

Four

I looked at him, and Raiden looked back at me. Neither of us moved.

I remembered, after the light there had been a hand, too tight on my wrist as it pulled me skyward. Cold and brittle, just like a skeleton. But Skeletons don't have flesh, or beating, breaking hearts. They were just dead, the rest of their existence rotted away, leaving only their bones. No sooner had that thought passed through my head then Raiden's cryptic words from earlier echoed after them.

"Last night you died."

I looked down at my hands. They were still perfect, still showing no signs of their previous mauling. This time I half expected to see my skin decaying before my eyes, but nothing happened until they began to blur. I blinked, and then hot tears splashed down on the forgotten quilt. I had no idea why I was crying, because at that moment I felt nothing. I was numb. Maybe I was really dead inside. As the panic rose in me at the thought of being stuck that way forever, I welcomed it.

"Ugh," Raiden groaned.

"Don't cry! That isn't even the worst of it!"

Not the worst of it? The panic escalated as I swatted at my tears.

I tried to stand but accomplished nothing. I was tired of Raiden looking down at me, and at some point, my legs had forgotten how to hold my weight and I fell—never hitting the floor. Raiden caught me by the same arm as before, and quickly pulled me up to face him.

He was taller than I remembered. My head barely reached his shoulders, which were so, so close. The musky scent from before began to overwhelm me when I noticed that his lips were close too, and they were moving again.

He released his grip on my arm, but he never stopped touching me. I could still feel the warmth of his fingers where they had dug into me as he stopped my fall—warm fingers —which reminded me nothing of the bony ones from the lake.

"You're warm, and skeletons are only bones."

Those were facts, no matter how incoherent they sounded coming out of my mouth.

"I can show you," he said.

I had no idea what he meant by that, but I was already agreeing.

"Come with me?" he asked in a whisper.

He was already pulling me out the door. His breath on my cheek lingered longer than I thought about not following his lead.

After the black walls of Raiden's room, the cheery yellow hallways were almost painful to look at. The walls were all lined with pristine white molding. No dust, no dents. I had a hard time believing this was even the same house. After everything I had heard today, believing that Raiden's bedroom door was some kind of portal to another dimension would not be a stretch.

Out of the corner of my eye, I noticed something reflective. I whipped my head around too quickly, the momentum of it nearly sent me to the ground. In a frantic second, I expected to see the lake there, but it was just a large mirror in an antique silver frame. It was polished to perfection and I didn't even glance at it. I was busy looking at the horrid sight in front of me.

Randomly, I thought, *At least I still have all my skin,* but that wasn't at all comforting.

Half my dark hair stuck flat to my head, and the other half was a frizzy mess. My lips were pale, and a line of thick dried blood sat in the creases—I couldn't work out what injury it was from. Then there was something out of place. There was a ring of gold around my irises but when I leaned in to get a better look I could no longer make it out.

The spell was broken, I looked down and saw I was wearing someone else's clothes.

"Where are my clothes?" I asked my reflection.

Raiden, who had been trying to pull me further along, turned back to face me. For the first time, I swore I saw him blush.

"What your run through the woods didn't shred, the lake had for dinner."

I failed to breathe. Did that mean that...?

"When you found me, was I... naked?"

"Marlow," he breathed, hot on my face again. "When I found you, you were nothing but bones."

We managed to make it out of the house without meeting anyone else, though I had a feeling there were others there, watching. Alex, and Lena—whose clothes I had on at the very least. There were other houses around the lake, none of them matched, and they all seemed to come from different times and places. The one that Raiden lived in was a faded blue and white beach house. I had seen dozens of them when I used to vacation on the East Coast. The one that was directly across from it had a distinctly Asian feel to it, and besides that there was a cottage, a brick colonial, and other structures I couldn't even place.

The sun had come up by then, and against the January snow it was more blinding than any ceiling fan could ever be. Raiden started down a long pier and I stared down at my feet. They were still bare. Old boards wailed under our combined weight. This was not the same dock as before.

"I found you across the lake," he said, pointing almost directly in front of us.

So he hadn't found me because I had practically washed up on his doorstop. He had been out in the night as well.

The end of the dock made an L, and Raiden sat on the bend. I slowly positioned myself next to him. His head hung heavy, like he had much on his mind, too much to say. His eyes were closed, his neck slack, he would have *looked* dead if not for the steady rise and fall of his chest.

Raiden sat to my right, and when the wind kicked up, his body blocked most of the spray from me. Wetness pulled away from the newfound waves of the formerly glassy lake and sailed through the air like slanted rain drops. I watched as they landed on his shirt and pants. There was no pattern in the mass of tiny circles.

Then I watched as they landed on his arm, and wrist, and fingers. They did not bead together or run off as real raindrops would. Instead, they seemed to shake before sinking into his skin. Then they began to glow that same blue which had forever been burned into my mind. From the moment I had seen that eerie mass in the lake, I knew it would stick with me for the rest of my life— no matter how short I thought it might be at the time.

The sight I was focused on now was something else entirely. The droplets that had permeated his skin had bled into large blue patches. Those patches revealed, through now completely opaque skin, nothing but bones.

No flesh, no blood. Nothing but shades of that ever-familiar blue, and sharp lines not rounded out by tissue and fat. When Raiden raised his head to look at me, I could see where the lake water had managed to splash on his face. I could look at his teeth in his jaw, and a space just above his right brow. I could, but all I was looking at were his eyes.

They were the same blue as the bone fragments peeking out from his translucent skin. Even more absurdly blue than they had been in his bedroom. I never looked away, not even when he grasped my fingers. His hand was still warm except for the three blue blotched fingers which felt like ice.

Raiden pulled me closer to the water's edge. I wanted to protest. I needed to pull myself back and just sit next to him until I really did just rot to dust. At least I didn't want to run away, and that seemed to surprise him too.

I did not resist as he used his other arm to angle me toward the warm waves. I didn't even flinch when he dipped my arm in up to my elbow.

Five

I had broken my right arm when I was seven. I remember the doctor holding up my x-ray to the light. How odd my bones had seemed then, and how broken. Now they were mended, but to me they still seemed so flawed. At some point I had grown to regard Raiden's blue light as beautiful, and now I stared at my own light which seemed dull by comparison. My muddy bronze lacked the intensity of his color, like I could blend into the dawn.

Raiden carefully pulled me up out of the water, returning me to my place next to him. Instead of the water dripping down my arm and toward the dock, it somehow crept upward. It was hot. When my arm had been submerged, the water had felt pleasant, just how it had been last night. Out of the water it burned like acid, searing across my skin. Eventually I glowed from the top of my shoulders down.

At any other time, seeing my bones would certainly signal a disaster, followed by a doctor's visit, and a lengthy recovery. This was so surreal. The sight of my bones didn't terrify me. I didn't seem wrong or grotesque to myself. Was I even the same self I was last night?

Rubbing the transparent expanse that encased my bronze glow was so odd. It felt exactly the same, as if my normal skin were still there. *Was it?* I had so many questions and that was not the most complex. I was amazed at how the effect transferred to my once dry left hand with such a small touch. I sat there, watching as my life line faded away. Wondering what had happened to me that I considered this entertaining and not horror film worthy.

"Let's go swimming," Raiden said.

He was serious again. He wanted us to go

swimming in a lake in the middle of the winter. I knew from personal experience that we wouldn't freeze in the warm currents, but it still seemed such a bizarre thing to do. After all, it had killed me.

Raiden stood and discarded his shirt before I agreed to anything. He walked to the edge of the dock and grinned back at me, and in a heartbeat, he was gone. He didn't even make a splash.

Careful not to get too close to the edge, I peered into the water, scanning the waves for the glow I was sure would be there. When I did not immediately see him and his bright light, I had to wonder how deep the lake was. Cautiously, I scooted a bit closer to the water, which was a mistake. In that second, one skeleton hand reached from the water and grabbed my ankle.

As I flew ungracefully toward the water, I did not think that my parents were probably worried out of their minds or any of my other thousand questions about my new existence. I only cared that I was about to get wet.

I hadn't given much thought to what being in the lake again would do to my psyche. This time, when the water came rushing into my ears, it was different. Instead of cutting off all the noise, it seemed to make the sounds from the lake sharper. I could hear hundreds of tiny noises, including my own limbs as I swung them in front of my face.

Hypnotized by the glow of my new body underwater, it seemed like I had only a moment to completely take it in before the blue light was again next to me. Raiden touched my face with the same fingers that had felt like ice on the dock. Now they were almost hot enough to burn. A burn I liked.

I wanted to hate him, but I hated myself more.

I wish I had known him better before today, and how odd it was that I felt I knew him now. He was still him, here with his bones showing, just like the guy I walked past every day in the hall before class. Since I had awoken earlier, I felt pulled to him in ways I didn't even know were possible. I was afraid of it, and desperately clinging to it at the same time.

Birds of a feather, my mother used to say.

She'd meant my friends were all no good, and that if I kept it up, I'd be the same.

I floated back to the top for air, but Raiden pulled me slowly back below the surface. I didn't want to stop the feeling of his bones on mine. I was in too deep.

Raiden's hands slid up to my face and down around my back. I knew exactly what he intended to do but I wouldn't allow it. I wanted it. I needed it.

Somehow, I knew when Raiden kissed me it would be like locking lips with a live wire. We should have been free floating. I didn't even notice how expertly, magically, he seemed to keep us in the same place, or that he had yet to need air the whole time he had been in the lake. I just let myself get shocked by his touch again and again. My body responded to his so well that I wouldn't have been surprised to find invisible veins locking us together as one. It was terrifying.

Eventually, when my air gave out, Raiden followed me back to the surface. I was astonished to see someone else standing by the lake. I tensed immediately but remembered Raiden has said regular people couldn't see the lake. I wondered if they saw two skeletons swimming in a cornfield or if we were hidden as well. Then I noticed the man's eyes focused on the disturbance we were creating in the lake. He was too far away for me to get a good look.

"Wait on the dock," Raiden said. "I'll be right back."

He pulled himself out of the water in one fluid motion. It took me several tries before I escaped and lay panting on the old wood. Raiden had already walked all the way back to land by the time I sloshed onto the planks.

When I looked down at my attire, I was amazed to see the lake had physically eaten away at my borrowed clothing. Was the secret to the lake as simple as acid?

The man bent down and whispered something in Raiden's ear. I watched his jawbone move as my name floated through the air. He raised one skeleton finger and pointed toward his house. I guessed he meant he would be back in a minute.

"Don't drown," he shouted over the waves.

I rolled over to watch him until he disappeared behind a doorway. Then I turned my attention back to the lake. My bones still glowed bronze beneath my see-through skin. I hadn't had that much time to experience myself alone below the surface and rising sun. I remembered the feeling of being weightless in the tempered lake water, and Raiden had only told me not to drown. Not to avoid the water entirely.

This time, I did my best to copy Raiden's elegant dive. I couldn't be sure how it looked to spectators, but it felt infinitely better to me. Swimming to a decent level, I stopped and let myself drift.

I didn't even consider how long I had been in the lake. Amazed at how I could so easily lose track of time while not breathing, my anxiety flared with frightening speed. I should stop wandering into easy traps. Especially the ones I set myself.

At least this time I would not need saving. With one bronze stroke after the next, I paddled my way to the top. In my short time under the water the sun had hidden itself behind a wall of dark clouds. From several feet below, I could almost see the intensity of the waves increasing.

Almost there, I shot one bony hand out into the air in a final frantic stroke. I could practically feel the anxiety ebbing away from my exposed fingers and down my arm.

I could feel my whole skeleton body relax as I greedily gulped down cold January air. Then two skeleton hands grasped me at my knees and pulled me back under.

Six

I kicked and jerked in an effort to get myself free, but it was useless. I was caught in a skeleton grasp that might as well have been shackles. Raiden's touch had been so gentle before, almost hesitant. This hold was demanding, hostile. I twisted around violently. My glowing bones cracked and popped in protest, but at least it caused me no pain.

When I did manage to get a good look, I found the skeleton trying to pull me into the darkness was different. Not fantastical, not alight. I had thought it was impossible to be any darker than the bottom of the lake. I couldn't even make it out from where I was, even if my vision seemed clearer than before. This being didn't shine with an eerie light—it seemed to suck what little light there was into it.

My mind was on the verge of breaking down. I had seen a stream of frightening things in the last few hours, but none of them had been out to get me. Nothing else had caused terror in me like this. Not even death. I couldn't look away, this creature seemed so empty. Was it a person even? Like me? Like Raiden? Was I even still a person?

I did not want to think about that. Nor did not want to think about drowning—or fear. They were both so near to consuming me.

The creature suddenly let go.

Never moving my eyes from his menacing ones, I slowly made my way back to the top. Faster and faster I paddled, as he seemed to be following me. Stalking me. That was when I heard it—the same cruel laugh as when I had drowned. Erupting around me as it came from everywhere and nowhere at the same time. I was sure it was from the monster below me.

Maybe this was Death, and he was angry that I had escaped him last time.

I broke the surface and managed to pull myself onto the dock in one try. I did not stick around to give myself a mental high-five. I stumbled into a running position and prepared myself to sprint. I thought about the distance to the blue beach house. I did not have that far to go. I took one miserable step and slammed into Raiden's chest.

He was completely dry and looked like he had in the house. No bones, nothing but the blue streak on his shirt where I had dripped on him to remind me of what was lurking just below the waves.

"There is something in the water," I rasped out.

It somehow sounded steadier than I would have thought possible. I considered how long I had been without air and was amazed that my lungs didn't even burn. Raiden was already watching the water. Eyes steady.

"I know," he whispered.

"You knew?" I asked.

"You knew there was a monster in the lake and you didn't think to tell me?"

He looked back at me again, pain and sadness clearly showing on his face. I felt my anger dripping away. Just like the lake water pooling below my feet. It dripped off my poor borrowed and ruined clothing.

"I didn't know he was there until I saw he wasn't in the house."

My mind spun around as if this dock was a ship out at sea and I was on the deck about to faint. It seemed like no matter what else was going on, I could not completely remove my thoughts from the boy in front of me.

Why would anyone keep a monster in the house?

Raiden released me gently, like he didn't really want to let go. I wondered how I ever could have thought that violent thing in the lake was him. He strolled down to the end of the dock confidently and called out to the open water.

"Get up here, you worthless Hollow!" he demanded.

His voice was no louder than he had been before, and again I heard that terrible laugh.

It's hard to describe the difference to a normal person—someone who thinks a skeleton is a skeleton and dead is dead. But I could tell the thing rising out of the lake was very different from Raiden and me. This monster was a bag of bones. His skin was still see-through, it was tinged a disgusting color similar to curdled milk. The worst part of it was the gaping hole in his chest.

His lungs did not expand to let in air, his heart did not beat. Both shook with his dark persistent laughter. I watched as his jaw flapped with it, and he was even more frightening than he had been in the lake.

When he had completely risen, I was immediately thankful I had Raiden standing between the two of us, and even more thankful that he did not seem afraid.

"So," said the monster, throwing his skeleton hands on his hips. It was almost comical looking. Like he was just some sort of distorted prop being jerked around hastily by a horrific puppet master.

"Is this the replacement?"

SEVEN

Raiden didn't respond. He stomped up to the grotesque skeleton and punched it in the face. Its bones rattled, and his whole frame trembled and shook, but it never ever stopped laughing.

"Replacement what?" I asked.

They didn't hear me and I felt intrusive, standing there so close to where they began to fight on the dock.

And how they fought. Like they intended to kill each other. Was this skeleton from the lake our enemy? He was cold and vicious. He was terrifying. There was something odd about the way they tried to tear each other apart, like pounding on your best friend because he stole your girlfriend.

I felt movement sending vibrations through the boards beneath me. I hadn't heard the shouting over the *click click* rattles from the fight. It was the same man from before. He was middle-aged and out of breath as he raced past me and grabbed Raiden by his trunk. He dragged him away from the skeleton that was still throwing punches.

"Conrad!" the man bellowed, "Enough!"

The laughing skeleton collapsed in a heap of bones at the end of the dock.

"Why, father?" the skeleton asked.

He shook his skeleton head, before speaking again.

"He started it, even if you won't believe me."

This man was this monster's father? I looked over the man again. The water from the others had wet parts of his shirt and lit up trails of silvery-blue. There must not have been a family resemblance.

"He's right," Raiden agreed.

"I started it. But he deserved it."

They scowled at each other.

"Aww, Dad!" Conrad said mockingly.

The monster sloshed water out of some of his hollow bits. I watched in horror as some ran *through* him.

"You run along inside and let me and the prodigal finish this like men!"

His father did not back down. Secretly, I was grateful. As much as I would never admit it to him, or anyone else, I had been worried Raiden had been about to lose that fight.

"Yeah Conrad, keep talking and you'll have to go retrieve your jaw from the bottom of the lake after someone else puts the rest of you back together. Though, I can't imagine who would bother. I wouldn't."

Conrad rushed Raiden, but his father stood his ground. Neither seemed like they wanted to hurt the man, but they were both clearly flustered by his presence. I thought I could smell blood mingled with lake water. I didn't even know if skeletons could bleed, and at that time I didn't want to know.

"Sure, old man, protect the perfect little boy you should have had! Wouldn't want to hurt his pretty, perfect, little face. Oh wait—yes I would."

It was odd, I realized—that Conrad's father worked so hard at protecting someone from his own son. That he would need to. Though perhaps he could see his son was a monster, it wouldn't be hard.

"Raiden is your brother!" the old man shouted.

I couldn't believe him. I couldn't believe Raiden could be related to Conrad because Raiden wasn't a monster, and because Conrad had made it so crystal clear that Raiden was not this man's son. It would have explained so much if it had not made so little sense.

"He's not my real brother! He's just some dying brat you took in because your kid was a freak!"

"Conrad," the man pleaded softly. "You know that's not true. You know why we need him. You know how it is, and you know he was never your replacement."

Replacement. There was that word again. My head swam. It felt as though I had jumped back into the lake. This man was

Conrad's father. Conrad who was a monster, admittedly so—and Raiden who was—or was not his brother. They needed him for something, by the sound of it, very important. Raiden was not the replacement. I was the replacement, but the replacement *what*?

I had been trying to keep myself from drowning in my own head. Swimming against deadly currents, I began to flounder. I hadn't realized they had stopped. I hadn't known they all were staring at me.

Raiden was streaked with electric blue, where Conrad had transferred wetness from the lake onto him. He was frowning at me. His matching blue eyes conflicted. Conrad's father wore a similar expression and I could tell, even though he was only curdled skin and blackish bones, Conrad was smiling. Smiling, right at me. I really wanted him to look away.

"You didn't tell her," he teased.

Pleased as if he had just come up with the joke of a lifetime. His bulging eyes never looked away from mine, and I could tell he was really speaking to Raiden.

"She has only just arrived here, son. That is a conversation for another time."

I knew nothing of this world I had unwittingly thrust myself into. I had been so unexpectedly drawn to a boy I hardly knew, and that was quickly consuming my whole head. Clogging any hope of rational thought, or concerns, or questions. I was suddenly furious with myself, and more than a little miffed at Raiden. Clearly, there was much more he should be telling me, but the conversation still needed to happen.

Huffing, I again looked for Raiden's eyes. They had narrowed. I had no doubt he already knew what was on my mind.

"I know when she got here!" Conrad spat.

"I saw her in the lake, remember?"

Yes, I had remembered him there too. Laughing, as he was now, as he seemed to almost always be. Raiden had pulled me out of the water, and at the time I hadn't realized they were not one in the same.

"You were *so* lucky wonder-boy Raiden was there to save you! If it had been up to me, I had left you there to rot, and trust me, I would have been doing you a favor. Why rehash the same things all over, if she is just going to meet the same miserable end as the last one?"

In my shock, I hadn't realized that Raiden had moved at all. I jumped when his fist connected with Conrad's face for a second time. Now the man was protecting Conrad. Something had snapped inside Raiden. There was desperation that had not been there in the first round. Eventually, their father did get them separated again. Panting hard, he would not relinquish his grip on Raiden.

"You will have to excuse my dear, dear foster brother," Conrad sang.

His smile was still plastered in place, and his eyes bulged in my direction. If Raiden didn't punch him again, I thought I might.

"Clearly," he continued in his condescending tone, "his dead ex is a bit of a sore spot for him."

Eight

All three of them hit the dock with a nauseating crunch. I was unsure if it was bones, or wood, or both. I seemed to remember seeing Raiden with a girl at school but that was before I paid him any attention at all. They often stood shoulders touching casually in the hall or sat pressed against each other at lunch. She had been petite, even shorter than me. I was almost positive her name had been Cassie or Cassandra or something, but that had seemed so long ago.

The thing I remembered most about her was her bright orange hair. I wouldn't have called that exact shade pretty if you had asked me before, but it made a fiery halo around her face, setting off her delicate features and many freckles. Somewhere down in the most broken part of me, my self-consciousness rekindled. She had been beautiful in a unique way I could never hope to achieve, and she had Raiden first.

She was also dead.

The boys were still fighting on the dock, so I swallowed down a million fears and ran forward. I had no idea if they would hurt me. I was almost positive Conrad would welcome the chance. I had to risk it. I had to know everything, and I was only coming up with more questions standing on the sidelines, watching them and doing nothing.

I reached out and touched Raiden's shoulder. Distracted, he looked up and Conrad kicked him in his gut. The air rushed out of him in one big gust. My intervention had hurt him, but it had also afforded their father the brief time he needed to again seize Conrad and, this time, drag him back toward the house.

That was when I noticed the wet streaks

on the man's shirt had grown. A reminder, that none of them were human.

But I guess, neither was I.

Tell me everything, I wanted to say. *Tell me anything I need to know.* All I could manage was, "What happened to Cassie?"

It came out colder than I intended, and it took everything I had to keep my voice from shaking. I stared down at my hands. It was becoming a bit of a habit. I was relieved to see that the fleshy tone to my skin was returning. I was sure I looked like some kind of molting leper. Raiden didn't seem to notice. He was staring out toward the open water of the lake.

I wanted to tuck the strands of hair that swirled around his ears in place. I wanted an excuse to touch him again. The idea made me cringe.

"She died," he said flatly.

He took a breath, and it sounded like it hurt. Before I could word the question, to demand the gruesome details he whispered, "She killed herself."

I gasped. I didn't want to, but I did before I could stop. I didn't want to make a sound, to break him anymore. I didn't know if I could live with myself if I caused him more pain. Selfishly, it seemed like hurting him was the same as hurting me.

More than anything I wanted to hate her, needed to. Because she had died and stayed that way, because she had left him alone and that made him miserable, and because no amount of anything I had to give would ever take that away. I wasn't the only selfish one, she had been too. Selfish people take their own lives and leave everyone else behind to deal with the aftermath. They lose. It was no different than what I had nearly achieved last night, even if I had seemed unaware of it at the time.

I tried not to blink. I could feel pools of tears forming in my lower eyelids.

"Everyone thinks the lake has given you to me. Some sort of peace offering... and I am so drawn to you. I've been slipping since the moment you opened your eyes and I am more disgusted with myself then you could ever know. I wanted to hate you for her, Marlow. Hate you for her memory that I have betrayed so many times already today."

Salty rivers raced down my cheeks, searching swiftly for the lake below my feet.

"But I can't. I can't hate you, Marlow."

I shook so hard my teeth rattled. I wrapped my arms around myself, trying to keep me all together. It wouldn't stop the sound. "How can you say those things to me?" I demanded. "I don't know anything. I just found out I died and came back a monster!"

"You aren't a monster."

"I don't know that! All I know is that something about you is consuming me. I don't think I could quit you even if I wanted to. I feel like I am playing some game where I forget to breathe. Please tell me why."

"Because you're mine."

"So you say!" I shouted back, "But what does that even mean? I am not a prize to be handed over. Am I doomed to follow you around like a little lost dog, waiting for you to throw me a bone or let me breathe you in?"

I took a step closer to him, he turned to face me. I didn't know if I intended to embrace him, or hit him.

"Of course not," he said defensively. "Marlow, I feel the same way about you."

I stopped. I didn't think it was possible for him to feel like this. Equal parts confusion, fear, need, and lust, fought for priority. Chaos. Each emotion hopelessly entangled.

"Tell me everything," I said, sitting back down on the dock.

He slid a hand onto my knee as he sat down beside me. Every time he touched me I wondered why he ever stopped. His eyes met mine, and I could tell he didn't really want to stop either.

But he did.

"I swear on whatever has become of my life that I will."

"Now?" I asked.

He shook his head.

"Why?" I asked.

"Because your parents are on their way to pick you up."

My old existence suddenly crashed back into me. Who had I even been before I had washed up on the shore of Skeleton Lake? Before I had died?

My parents were going to kill me. I

hadn't called. I'd snuck out. I hadn't called. I had been missing since yesterday, and I hadn't called.

"What should I say?"

"To who?" Raiden asked.

"My parents."

"Oh. Well, dad already told them the truth. We figured it was the easiest way."

A nervous laugh tickled the back of my throat.

"You thought telling my parents that I died, and came back a swimming, lusting skeleton was the easiest way? What was the hard way? Is it to early to scream April Fool's and take it all back?"

Raiden laughed swiftly, his smile quickly faltered, like he had again remembered something sad. He even blushed.

"I meant," he said. "I meant that he told them what happened at the party. He led them to believe you came here to spend some time with Lena. Since you were so distraught and all, I doubt they will hold it against you."

He looked so embarrassed. I could tell he didn't want to rehash this any more than I did.

"You were upset," he noted. "But the further you are from that piece of demon trash the better... though at least you are of no use to him now."

"You called him that before. A demon, like, a *real* demon?" I wasn't sure I believed in demons, but I didn't believe in living skeletons either.

He titled his head to the side as he looked back at the lake.

"You'll see."

NINE

We pulled ourselves off the dock as the air tingled. The friction was tangible, the air and emotions were all too real. We did not go back to the blue house. Instead we went right, and started slowly around the lake.

The wind still blew, and the smell of the lake water permeated the rest of my senses. As I walked beside Raiden I wondered if I would always be so aware of it. I wanted to reach out and take his hand, but I was almost sure if I did I would lose whatever drive I had to seek answers.

Raiden seemed deep in his own struggle, though I doubted his involved hand holding.

As we approached the next closest house, he slowed his pace. I watched him open his mouth as if to speak, only to close it again, like he had thought better of it.

I wanted to encourage him to continue. To tell him I needed to hear whatever he had to say, but I didn't have the right words either. I gave up and took his hand instead.

We were both dry, and he felt warm and safe. He didn't recoil, or even flinch. He squeezed my fingers tighter, like I was the sturdy one.

I didn't have time to question my decision to give in, because my hand in his seemed to give him the push he needed to say what he needed to.

"I wish there was time to tell you—"

"Everything?" I asked.

"Everything. It's not like I set out to intentionally keep things from you. I don't even know where to start," he sighed.

I believed him. I could feel the truth of his words like they were seeping into my blood through my fingertips.

The sun had fully risen while we were on the dock. It felt lovely and warm as it shone on my face. The lake managed to heat the air immediately around it, so I had no need for a coat. It was pleasant, like a giant space heater. Damp grass and soft ground lay below my feet. The wind blew, but here it was without its typical January bite.

"My parents are never going to let me out of their sight after this," I said.

"I'll see you Monday at school, definitely."

School! I had completely forgotten Raiden and I went to the same school, that I even knew of him before. I guess I would be kissing that perfect grade I had in history goodbye.

"And after that?" I asked. "So we can talk."

"You can come whenever you want. Really, this should be your home now but—"

"But?"

"We've never had a local before."

"Where were you from before?"

"Boise," he replied. "But I don't remember it."

Selfishly, I didn't want to go back. I wanted to plant my feet into the cool earth, and have Raiden tell my parents I had stayed dead, to never leave him. I knew how much that would hurt them, how much I had already hurt them. So I kept walking.

Raiden paused when we reached a large farm house. It was the only house at the lake that looked like it belonged in Iowa at all. It had a yellowing back porch. Large patches of the white paint on the house were cracked and peeling because of the sun, or how close it was to the lake, or maybe just for authenticity.

"This is the only house the humans can see," Raiden mentioned over his shoulder.

Somehow I had known that already.

He dropped my hand, and the absence made me feel cold from the inside out. I had all too easily developed an addiction to him. It seemed both scary and necessary to me at the same time.

I watched as Raiden ran up the back steps, like he had hundreds of times. Likely he had. He knocked on the old and faded screen door, which I was almost positive was solely for my benefit.

A woman opened the screen. She smiled

at Raiden in an odd sort of way, something motherly, but something else.

There was something about her that seemed familiar, but I couldn't place it.

Lena walked past the woman and pulled me inside. I assumed this was her mother. This was the first time I had been around Lena since I had been pretending to sleep in Raiden's bed. I knew this girl, but she went by Laura at school.

She didn't mention it, while she pulled me through a doorway that ended up being her bedroom, not even looking sideways at her clothes I had managed to ruin. Typical for this residence, I guessed.

Her room was painted a purple pastel. The curtains were white eyelet and lace. It was fit for a princess, aged five.

She sighed. "It's been this way since I was three, and it would break my mother's heart if I changed it. Besides, we don't let fleshies over, and no one else cares."

Fleshies, I supposed was a non-flattering word for human, which I had been up until last night. I nodded, but she had already turned to slam the door in Raiden's face. Up until then he had been loitering in the doorway.

"No boys!" she teased.

"That's not what you said last night," came a muffled voice from the other side of the door.

I had a feeling that voice belonged to Alex, though I hadn't actually seen him in the house.

"Really!" she shot back. "Good luck with that." She winked at me, and her eyes looked strange. I'd have said they were violet.

Lena dove in to her top drawer, and came back up with a pair of yoga pants, a white t-shirt with long sleeves, plus the tiniest thong I had ever seen. I blushed. "Hold on," Lena said, looking for something else, hopefully a bit more substantial.

She came back, and added a sports bra to the pile of borrowed clothing. I lunged for it. I would deal with the thong if it meant not feeling like my breasts were exposed by my tattered clothing.

"Change," she told me. "I'm going down the hall to get the details on your parent's arrival. Hurry."

This time she closed the door quietly behind her. It felt good to be alone. I wanted to savor it, and not think of anything else. I could break down in my own room later. I was supposed to be hurrying. Given my luck, my parents were already pulling up and seeing nothing but this old farm house in an empty field. No skeletons, no lake.

Ignorance is sanity, I thought as the doorbell rang.

I wish I had not made the mistake of checking my reflection on the way out. I looked like a girl who had just died. At least I wouldn't have to work hard at making my parents believe I was irrationally upset. My hair did that just fine. Judging by my appearance, I had never been so irrationally upset in my life.

Opening the door, I stepped into Lena.

"Your dad's here," she hissed. "Raiden went home. Best not to bring him up."

No problem, I thought. None whatsoever.

TEN

The ride home was excruciating. It felt longer than anything at the lake did. The only consolation was the discovery that Lena's house was really only ten minutes from mine. I wondered how many times I had been by it and seen nothing. I imagined what it would be like to walk there in the summer time, with wild flowers and green grass making a soft carpet below my feet. No ice to chill me, no snow to drift around my soul.

I shivered.

To my father's credit, he didn't say a word. Thankfully, devoid of the lake water, my skin had resumed its normal, pasty hue.

Could my father have seen my bones? Would the sight of his daughter bronze and bright terrify him? Or, would it be like the lake itself and he would simply be unable to?

I pressed my cheek against the cold fogged up window of the passenger's seat. I wanted to stay awake. I was unsure what I would dream of if I closed my eyes. Once I was asleep I would have no control. I could dream of pretty blue eyes, or monsters from the deep, dragging me under and pulling me into the holes in their hearts.

At some point I lost my fight. Even before we started past the land that made up our nonworking farm, there was only darkness. My father woke me after pulling into our circle drive with a shake. At least there had been no nightmares.

I trudged up the stairs to the front porch. The too-bright green my mother had painted them last summer flaked onto the snow below my feet. No one noticed but me. Mom was staring at me through the kitchen window like I might break. I knew she had no idea why. I felt cold, conflicted, like maybe

I no longer belonged to the place I called home.

Raiden had invaded my heart. My very existence was full of him—false flesh and bronze bones. I couldn't let him live here, permeating the walls of my family home. So I did my best to push him out of my mind. It would have been impossible if I hadn't been almost immediately met with a distraction. It would be impractical to think I would have gotten off scot free but I had been harboring high hopes.

As it turns out, the punishment was pretty inconsequential, all things considered.

Two weeks of very lax grounding. I probably could have had the time reduced if I had dared to open my mouth and argue. They almost looked like they wanted me to do it. I couldn't. The whole conversation had been awkward, and I had no desire to drag it out longer than necessary.

Once properly (though reluctantly) sentenced, my parents allowed me to retreat back to the confines of my own room. I could feel their pitied stares on my back, and on my mind, long after I had made it all the way up the stairs.

My room always smelled of musty old quilts and my favorite spearmint gum. I used to hate that no amount of body spray would take away that smell. Now, I welcomed it.

The room, which my parents jokingly referred to as "The Pineapple Express," had been my grandmother's hobby room until she died. She often said that there was no way a person could be unhappy surrounded by so many pineapples. Despite raising three kids, she must have not known teenagers very well. Even if she had, it probably wouldn't have stopped her from papering all four walls in miniature orange and green fruits.

Grandmother's wallpaper trend lasted for a few years, until grandpa had his first heart attack. The actual paper persisted still, fading over time like this whole town. I suppose grandma eventually realized there were some things in this world even pineapples couldn't fix.

I flung myself down on my bed, with its old worn quilt that had belonged to my aunt. My knees popped like they never had before.

There was so much I needed to learn about this existence, but the most important thing I needed to learn was how to keep it a secret. The people, and the lake around it, seemed to have been around for a while. I was sure that I could totally ruin everything in just under five seconds.

Most of the day I slept on top of the covers, learning to like the cold air. My mother came to wake me for lunch. I wasn't ready to face my parents, so I went back to sleep.

When my father came to wake me for dinner, I could tell there was no refusing them or my stomach this time. I hadn't eaten since last night, which was a lifetime ago in my mind.

As quietly as possible, I snuck into the bathroom down the hall. I was having a shower before I attempted conversation, and I did not want them to have time to object. I drew my remaining moments of isolation out as long as I could. Eventually, I stepped into the chilly spray that felt wrong. I had enjoyed the coldness of my room, but the lake had been warm and this water was all wrong.

So, I adjusted the temperature, letting the water scald my neck and drip down my back. Looking down, I almost expected to see the glow of my bronze bones. Lake water, not tap water, was all that could reveal what I was convinced was certain. My flesh was false.

When all the hot water was gone from the old pipes, I reluctantly stepped out of the tub. Briefly, I thought of drying my hair, but then my parents would know there was really something wrong with me.

In my oldest jeans, and newest t-shirt, I did my best to walk down stairs like every-thing was fine. The boards creaked below my feet in a way that reminded me of the dock that had led me to end my previous existence. The smells and the other sounds however, were very different.

In the kitchen, I could hear my mother clanking around silverware as she set the table. They rattled and clanked in a way that was nothing like bones, and the constant hum of the decrepit refrigerator was a poor replacement for the moving water of Skeleton Lake.

My parents both looked up as I entered

the room. Concern seemed to be permanently etching its way into their faces, and I was hoping they still wouldn't want to talk about it. It was no longer even a blip on my emotional radar.

Luckily, again it seemed they had judged my state too fragile, and I never thought it would be so good to appear so weak. Instead of speaking to me directly, they opted for their usual small talk. They complained about the weather while forcing two helpings of beef stew into me. They ignored me as they gossiped about my mother's church friends, who would probably be gossiping about me by Monday. They completely avoided eye contact with me for the duration of the meal.

Per usual, after everyone was done, I began washing dishes by hand. The old farmhouse had never seen such modern conveniences as a dishwasher. I was surprised when my mother shooed me off. Not one to ever look an escape opportunity in the mouth, I dried my hands and fled.

But she managed to catch me before I got both feet on the bottom step.

"Marlow?" she called to me, over the sound of running water.

She was speaking quietly, and I had barely heard her. I wanted to pretend I hadn't at all. She sounded so pathetic; I couldn't bring myself to hurt her further.

"Just promise me," she begged, "you won't do this again."

Eleven

That night I woke and slept in fitful shifts, unsure of which darkness was worse: the fog of my constant nightmares, or the black behind my own eyelids. Even the semi-darkness of my own room felt like it was closing in.

Again I slept, and again I dreamed of beasts I couldn't see. I felt them, and I could hear the things they planned to do with me. In one end of my mind they seemed to be arguing. Some of these beasts, with their near human voices, wanted to gnaw the meat from my limbs as I withered in pain. Others wanted to skin the flesh from my pretty bones, and hang them as a warning.

They never said what the warning was for, but several of them called, "Take it back!"

"Take what back?" I asked the wind in my head.

Their fighting went on, and my ability to focus on them lessoned. I wasn't immediately aware of the orange blur next to me, then my mind flinched. It was a girl, as bright as a fire raging out of control. The intensity made her hard to see, but I knew her face.

Cassandra Hardin looked at me and sighed.

"They'd kill you if they got the chance," she huffed. "Don't give it to them."

I opened my mouth to ask her a million things, but all that came out was, "Are you a ghost?"

In a world where Skeletons are alive, and monsters lurk in the deep, I was sure the answer was going to be yes but she was only a dream. My beautiful and dead nightmare. She didn't want to kill me, just take back her boyfriend.

She laughed, and her voice sounded like the wind chimes on our porch in the summer.

"I'm only a memory," Cassandra said, smiling. But she wasn't my memory. I couldn't recall saying more than three words to her in my life. "I chose you from all the others," she sang. "To give you the life I gave away, to save you from sharing a fate with me. Don't make the same mistake again."

And she was gone in a wave of rain on my window.

"Rain," I mumbled, still half asleep. It was too cold for rain.

I pushed myself up to get a better look, and again the sound permeated my room. It wasn't rain, or even ice. It looked like clumps of snow and rocks. I was out of my bed with the window halfway up before I made the decision to move at all.

It had to be Raiden.

I grabbed last year's coat. My other jacket was still where I left it at the party. It fit snuggly and made climbing difficult. Somehow, I got out my window and onto a frozen tree branch.

For the second night in a row I was barefooted in the snowy outdoors. I could see the figure of a boy waiting just below me by the base of the tree. My heart seemed to rattle around in my rib cage as I ungracefully raced my way down the trunk.

When I meant to swing myself down from the lowest branch, I slipped, and waited for the teeth-shaking impact that never came. Two warm hands wrapped around my middle, and slowly lowered me to the ground. I looked up; expecting to see blue eyes, but dark ones stared back at me instead.

They were familiar somehow, but I was positive I had never seen this boy before. I wasn't afraid. He was every bit as gorgeous as Raiden was, but darker and seemingly more dangerous. He had curly dark locks that stuck up like art, and the bone structure of an Abercrombie model. He was pretty and rugged at the same time. He was too perfect to be lurking below my window.

With this beautiful stranger I felt guilty, like I was cheating on a boy I couldn't remember committing myself to. It was both frightening, and absurd.

"Who are you?" I whispered.

Then he smiled, and he didn't have to say

a thing because I knew. I had met this boy before, but that seemed impossible.

"Forgot me already, huh? Raiden has already got the stars in your eyes. He does that."

I nearly choked. "Conrad?" This beautiful boy didn't look at all like the beast I had remembered. That voice still haunted me. "How did you find me?"

"Easy." Conrad winked. "I followed you home. What? You didn't think you were the only one who liked to run though the wilderness, did you, Marlow?"

I didn't say a thing. I was caught up in the overwhelming desire to slap him, or maybe slap myself. I had been attracted to him!

"Leave me alone!" I shouted, backing up. I tripped over a buried tree root, and he tried to right me but I shrugged him off. "I don't want you here!"

"Look," he pleaded. "I know we got off on the wrong foot, but I wouldn't have really left you in the lake..."

I refused to say another word as I turned

my back to him and started up the tree. I thought about chancing the front door. My mother kept a spare key under the gnome statue in her rose garden. I'd never make it up the stairs without waking everyone in the house, though.

Eventually I made it. Conrad was laughing beneath me the whole time, likely waiting for me to slip so he could again play the hero. I tumbled into my room with all the stealth of an angry rhinoceros. I reached to slam my window shut, but he called up to me.

"Juliet!" he mocked. "Juliet!"

I glared back down at him. He looked far less intimidating from such a distance.

"What?" I demanded.

"Let's not go for a repeat on that last act, all right? You have no idea the kinds of things that are out there in the night. The things that ignored you when you were a frail, and fleshy human, will flock to you like moths to your pretty bronze light."

He was gone before I slid the window back in place.

———

I wished I had my snow boots, but they were at the bottom of the stairs. I laced up my Nikes instead. This time, before climbing out my window, I put on layers and a hat, and I dropped my coat from the ledge so it landed on the snow in a heap. I knew the extra bulk would only make it fit snugger, and I didn't want anything to hinder my limited climbing abilities. This time there would be no one around to catch me.

I nearly managed to slip on the same bit of ice, on the same tree branch as before, but this time I caught myself.

I landed on the ground with a familiar crunch. Last night I had climbed out the bathroom window, and onto the porch. It had shook like the whole structure might give way beneath me, and it sounded like it would too. I convinced myself the oak was easier.

Pulling on my coat, I searched for Conrad's footprints in the snow. There might be real monsters out there in the night, and I was almost positive he would know how to avoid them.

His tracks went north, through the remains of our neighbors cornfield. In the growing season, perfectly spaced rows would rise and fall with the hills. Tonight they stood bare and ghostly, even though the sky still stood devoid of the moon there was enough light to see skeletal plants popping up from where the snow had been blown away. I hurried. I didn't want anyone seeing me fleeing in the night. Not anyone or anything.

I had to see Raiden again. I had to know... I had to know.

Soon, the cornfields gave way to the woods. At first it was still easy to follow his path, but as the trees grew taller and closer together it became impossible and I convinced myself I wasn't lost until long after I was. I should have turned back, but my desire blinded me. I had been in these same woods last night.

At least, I thought they were the same.

Last night the lake had pulled me toward it. Perhaps it could lead me there again. I closed my eyes, and I felt emptiness. Panic spread through my veins like poison. I wanted to scream. I tried to clear my head. To let go of everything else, and for a moment there was nothing. No snow or trees, no frightening impossible circumstances, just the sound of my own breathing, in the darkness of my mind. I was safe.

"Don't say I didn't warn you," an orange light said.

Snap, went a branch to my right. My eyes flew open, there was nothing there. Only the sound of grating wood, like thick branches, crashing and withering against each other in the wind. Everything in the night was calm, except my own heart.

I turned around to follow my own confused steps out of the woods, but slammed into a tree I was sure wasn't there before. When I looked up, the tree was flesh covered, and humanoid.

Then it talked. Screwing words up in a disgusting hole of a mouth, like a knot in the middle of a rotten tree.

"Pretty bones," said the beast. He spit ruddy bark when he spoke, and it stuck to my clothes and hair. "Lovely bones."

It grabbed me. I wiggled and kicked, but it had me tight in its petrified grasp. There seemed no more hope fighting this tree than the oak in my yard. Maybe even less, and my oak had no intentions.

He dragged me through the woods by my arms, which I could no longer feel. I was sure both shoulders had been dislocated, and I was thankful no shooting pain accompanied that. It was a peculiar feeling being bumped along with your joints misaligned, like floating on a rickety raft.

In the beginning I screamed. Then I cried. It was no use. Conrad was long out of these woods. Tears had frozen to my cheeks and chin by the time he left me in a lump by the foot of a tree. I looked up in a daze, relieved to see it was a real one.

There was a fire a few feet away, but it did little to warm me. Standing in front of it were three more creatures, all as hideous as the first. I couldn't decide if they were more person or plant. Had they been born this way? Had something happened to them, like what happened to me?

"I say we eat her," said the largest and ugliest.

"I say we take her pretty bones and hang them as a warning. Those lake rats think they are so much better than us, keeping the magic for themselves!" bellowed the beast that had brought me here.

I was shaken out of my cold stupor. This was just what I had dreamed, only so much worse. I couldn't pull my eyes away, afraid that if I glanced in the wrong direction, they would seize the chance, and that would be the end of me. I had already made so many mistakes.

Drool dripped from their twisted mouths as they continued to argue with each other. They were distracted, and I realized I should run, but I didn't think I could even compose myself enough to stand.

I just wanted to see Raiden again. To tell him I was sorry. To do the exact thing that had lead me to this place, but I had only myself to blame for my stupidity.

My heart seemed to betray its playlist. *Thunk*. It went before a pause. *Thunk thunk*.

It felt like it might have dropped into my stomach. I clutched my chest trying to halt its erratic rhythm. It still sat where it should, and as it pounded below my fingertips I thought of the first time I had seen Conrad, when I had noticed the hole in his heart. Such a disgusting sight I thought it had been then, but my heart looked no different further in than skin deep.

Real hearts weren't pretty, but mine still managed to leap before I did.

When I looked up, I hadn't realized I looked away from the fire. The beasts now stood next to me.

At first I thought they had reached some kind of decision on exactly what torture awaited me. They were all facing me, mouths agape, though perhaps they always looked that way. They were so inhumanly still, I wanted them to stay rooted to the ground, and maybe become the trees they so closely resembled. That idea seemed ludicrous, but so did all the truths these days. I swatted at the ice below my eyelids, just as a hand touched my neck.

I opened my mouth to scream. Forcing air out of my lungs, ready to produce the loudest noise possible, and then I let out. But what tumbled out of my mouth wasn't a scream—it sounded like a song, but muddled. Like a siren singing underwater.

Shocked I clamped my mouth shut. The person who touched me was the man from the lake—Conrad's father.

He stood next to me, smiling in the darkness of the woods. Surrounded by creatures that wanted to separate me from whatever kept them from my bones. He smiled.

I was really starting to notice the family resemblance.

"If you had done that before," he chuckled. "It would have made it a whole lot easier to find you."

I wanted to ask him what he meant by that, but my voice was gone. Sandblasted and raw, my throat ached.

"No fair!" shrieked the beast that had dragged me away. "We found the girl, we keep the girl."

"You know better than to attack a guardian of Skeleton Lake! Now go or we'll evict you from the forest."

"You have no authority here, Abraham! This is our forest, and we do as we please."

So the man's name was Abraham. He was still smiling.

"I didn't say we'd just ask you to leave nicely."

TWELVE

"Raiden. I got her." Abraham spoke into a walkie-talkie. Raiden swore and chastised Conrad in response. They were together.

I cried harder as Abraham walked me through the woods. At least my arms seemed fine. Eventually the trees thinned, and I saw him. Raiden stood at the edge of the trees, his back faced me, and he was still yelling at Conrad, who was laughing as usual. I was reminded how much I wanted to slap him, but there was something more powerful moving me than anger.

I took the few steps separating us devoid of my own free will. I felt nothing until I felt his arms. It was like regaining feeling in a severed limb. I hadn't had any idea how much I had missed him. I should have been afraid. What had Cassandra really given me? All I could do was feel.

An old green army Jeep was parked out by the side of the road. Conrad and Abraham were up front. The elder man drove as Raiden and I sat crunched in the back seat.

They wanted to take me home. I wasn't ready. I was worried I would never be.

"I warned you not to leave," Conrad said from the passenger's seat.

"I know," I admitted. "I tried to follow you back, but I got lost in the woods."

Raiden looked like he wanted to fight with him again, but he was doing his best to bite his tongue. I wondered if they always fought like this or if I just bring out the worst in everyone.

We had been less than a quarter mile from the south side of the lake. I didn't know if I wanted to scream or cry but I didn't care, because Raiden was with me. I just hoped I wouldn't have to spend the rest of my life chasing after him.

Then I remembered Cassie, and my smile faltered. I could tell by the puzzled look in Raiden's eyes that he had seen me momentarily slip, and was searching for the cause. How do you tell someone, especially someone that you might be in love with, that their dead ex-girlfriend haunts your dreams and speaks to you in your nightmares?

I wondered if he knew, and if he had all along. I had now realized that Cassandra's gift had affected me in ways I couldn't even begin to understand. I could spend the rest of my life under this spell, and I still wouldn't think it was a bad thing. I never wanted it to fade, but I supposed all things do with time.

Finally, there was the lake house again.

Raiden led me inside, and helped me to shed my coat. Abraham didn't even watch as we scampered back to his room.

When the door shut behind us, Raiden's face was more somber. He looked at me with wide, blue eyes, and I realized he had been afraid.

His room was exactly how it had been before. His bed was unmade, and I was reminded again of the late hour. He had likely been asleep before they went to go find me. "How did you know where I was?" I asked.

Raiden paced the small space. When he broke eye contact with me the temperature in the room plunged with the absence of his gaze. "I knew something was wrong." He paused. "Then Conrad came in and I heard him arguing with dad. He said he thought you had followed him into the woods."

He clenched his fist. I could hear every one of his knuckles pop, and I was reminded again of the hole in the wall.

"Marlow," he breathed, eyes returning to mine.

I liked the way my name carried through the air when he said it. I hated what he said next.

"I have never been so close to killing him in my whole life. And trust me; there have been a few very close calls."

I believed him. I also believed that it was just as likely Conrad would have emerged from that fight the winner. "Please don't talk like that, Raiden."

"Why did you come here, Marlow? I

know you want answers, but it was dangerous. You could have waited until Monday."

I shook my head. I wanted answers, but
that wasn't why I had been running here in
the dark. I took a step in his direction, then
two. "You," I whispered. "I just wanted you."

When his lips met mine, I felt as though
my whole body sighed. His left hand slid
from the space between my shoulders to the
small of my back, blazing a trail that did not
fade as it should as he increased the pressure.
As the force of his kisses tilted my head back,
the fingers of his other hand began to play
with the hem of my shirt.

I am positive it would have gone too far,
but as warm digits spread across my naval a
crash came from outside in the hall. I should
have thanked Conrad for his timely interrup-
tion, but in that moment I wanted him as
dead as Raiden did.

Loathing flashed through Raiden's eyes,
so fierce I couldn't stand to look at it. So I did
the only thing I knew how to end it. I pulled
him back to me.

I could feel the excitement flickering
behind his feverish kisses. Before, they had

been, in a way, familiar. Now they had returned to electrifying. I begged to be shocked again and again.

I wanted to pull him over to the bed. My hands held two fistfuls of his shirt, but he resisted. I could feel my ego crumbling, as what I had been trying to do began to overwhelm me even more than his skin did. I hadn't heard the soft knocking on the door, but Raiden had.

"Sorry," Abraham called through the door. "We should probably get her home before the sun comes up."

Thirteen

Raiden helped me up the tree and into my room. I thought hard about inviting him in, but there was a level I was willing to push my luck and I had exceeded it days ago.

I did watch him shimmy back down the tree, and then give me a wry smile before running back into the night. In my mind, I saw him running all the way back to his father's jeep. We had left it parked way down the dirt road. I looked out the window far longer than my vision was good for. Eventually, I collapsed back in bed. The hollow of my back was still warm where Raiden's hand had been. I relished in it until I could feel nothing at all.

I knew the minute I opened my eyes the next morning I had slept far too long. Sun poured into my room in mid-morning heaps, and dad liked to attend the seven thirty Mass. I hadn't closed the window last night. I wondered if anyone else had noticed how cold it had gotten upstairs.

Under ideal conditions the ancient furnace had to fight to warm the old farmhouse. Keeping the window open wide wasn't doing it any favors.

It was silent downstairs. My mind raced back to the horrid creatures from the woods and my heart beat down the same path. On the way back home Abraham had assured me that creatures like that did not go in the houses of men, even if I was in one. That did little to comfort me.

I untangled myself from my sheets still clothed. My bedroom door stood ajar, and I knew that wasn't how I left it last night. I had been one hundred percent sure that it was closed before sneaking out twice.

Pushing the old door out of my way I

stepped into the hall. The house remained still. I hoped, for the first time ever, they had left without me.

Not bothering to attempt silence on my way down the stairs, I sprinted down. I rounded the corner and stopped.

Lena was in my kitchen. Her white blond curls were pulled into a low ponytail, and it hung like a waterfall down her back. She stood facing away from me, drumming on the counter with the fingers of one hand, and flipping through the newspaper with the other. Her music was blaring so loud she didn't hear me come down. Lyrics were leaking out of her ear buds loud enough for me to hear every word.

I didn't bother calling her name. Sliding up to the counter I pulled one plug out of her ear. I expected her to be surprised, but she didn't even flinch.

"Sorry!" she apologized, plucking out the other ear bud. "I had no idea when you would be waking up!"

"Lena? How did you get into my house?"

"Your mom let me in on the way out the

door. Should she not have?" Her eyes looked hurt.

That hadn't been why I had asked at all. "It's okay." I smiled. "I'm just supposed to be grounded. I'm also supposed to be at church."

"Oh! Well your mom said you could use a friend, and I guess you must have needed a break after last night—" Of course Lena knew about last night. I was starting to believe everyone knew everything about me. "Do you have movie channels?" she asked, eyeing the television in the living room from her place by the counter.

As it turns out there are some things even Skeleton Lake can't give you. Things like HBO and Showtime.

I wanted to use our time alone to get some answers out of Lena, but that required knowing which questions I should ask. Not knowing where to start, I brought up the one subject Lena seemed to care about more than Cinemax—Alex.

She talked about everything about him. The first time she had seen him. She was older and had arrived at Skeleton Lake before he had. She even talked about the clothes they had worn to homecoming. Her dress was strapless and pale pink. She had even talked Alex into wearing a matching tie.

In my mind I could never picture Raiden agreeing to that, but I was more interested in how exactly they had all come to Skeleton Lake.

The television blared; it was nothing more than background noise to me. I knew that they had not been born here. Raiden had said he was from Idaho. When I asked Lena how they arrived at the lake her cheeks tinged red before she looked away. When she looked back at me, smiling, I thought for a bizarre moment she was going to say the stork had brought them.

"We were scattered all over to begin with," she said between movies. "But we all had one thing in common."

I was curious what magical thing could have possibly linked them all together when they all seemed so different.

"What?" I asked on cue.

"We were all young and—we were all dying."

"I'm sorry?" I squeaked.

But Lena completely misunderstood my meaning. Saying only that it was fine, it was a long time ago and she had been so young she hadn't really understood what was happening.

"No—I mean, you were dying? Or you are dying? Because you aren't—he's not, is he?"

I couldn't get my head to think that I could lose Raiden. Not when I had only just found him. Her face turned serious again, and I was amazed at how much that aged her girlish features. "Marlow, didn't Raiden tell you what happened to you in the lake?"

He had. That was one of the only things he had told me. "He said that I... died."

She shrugged, like death wasn't hard. Like death wasn't final.

"So it's always the same way then?"

She shook her head again. "It's usually the same way. We only have two anomalies. You and Conrad."

I didn't really like the sound of being called an anomaly, but I was too focused on prying information out of her frowning lips.

"Me?"

"Yes, you're old, and you're—"

"A replacement."

That was what Conrad had called me at the lake, and I knew now that it was true. Cassandra had saved me from my untimely death, giving me what she had wasted. The life that had saved her from her certain end as a child. She saved me from being a suicide, but she couldn't save me from the regret.

"And Conrad, why is he an anomaly?"

She looked like she was going to be sick and then looked at me intently. I watched as she chewed off all the lip gloss on her bottom lip.

"I'd rather you asked someone else about him, to be honest," she mumbled. "Actually, I probably shouldn't say anything else until you talk to Raiden and Abraham. I'll see you tomorrow at school, okay?"

She was running out the door before I could piece together why. I understood not wanting to talk about Conrad. I didn't really want to talk about him either. What had I said that had scared her away?

Fourteen

I dozed on the couch until my parents came home from church. We ate lunch. I did my homework as I pretended nothing was wrong. Pretended there was no hand-me-down romance making my hormones and head spin. Pretended there were no living skeletons in the closet.

I was fine.

I went to bed early and dreamed of awful Mondays. I imagined no monsters in the dark, no dead girlfriends on my mind. I ignored the fact that I was afraid. I pretended I wasn't.

I pretended a lot of things.

My alarm went off at six in the morning,

but I had been awake for hours. I had no idea what to wear, and less idea what to say and do. I had awoken mid-nightmare in a cold sweat, completely awake, and completely unaware of what I had been seeing in my dreams. The pineapple room still smelled like gum and decaying fabric, but it felt unfamiliar now.

The loose floorboard in front of my closet creaked and rocked as I couldn't make up my mind. Doing something so ordinary made me remember—a lifetime ago, I had made a fool of myself in front of a house full of people and, today, I'd have to do something about it.

My plan involved ignoring the general populous. I didn't care. Let them talk.

Cassie had never cared what everyone thought of her. I had only ever watched her from afar. I was starting to think that maybe she was stronger than I was, and I hated her for it. That sounded a lot better than hating her because she had Raiden first. She had thankfully kept out of my dreams, and I hoped that by accidentally signing up for this existence, I wasn't inviting her to follow me through it.

After a breakfast I didn't touch, I headed down my drive. The joys of country living. I couldn't wait to have children so I could tell them I had to walk uphill both ways in the snow to get to my bus stop. At least I wasn't barefoot this time.

I treaded mostly on the snow covered grass, avoiding the half frozen slush on the dirt road. As the hum from my house faded behind me, the only sound came from the crunching of frozen wetness under my boots.

When I made it to the edge of the main road, I stopped. There, almost exactly where it had been the night before last, was Abraham's green Jeep. I would have believed it had never moved, if not for the all the tracks leading there and away in the snow.

My breathing grew shallower. The cold air bit at my mouth and nose and I ran anyway. This time not because I hoped to escape something, I ran because I didn't want the feeling to escape me.

Abraham was nowhere in sight. Raiden

stepped out of the driver's side door as soon as I had reached his back bumper. He said something I missed as I slid into his arms. I didn't care.

"I missed you too," He mumbled into my hair.

I missed him too. Since Friday night, I had become hopelessly codependent. Lena's eyes glazed over when she talked about Alex, and I had a feeling that was just how it was for skeletons. She said there were always equal numbers. Everyone was meant for everyone else, and if destiny existed then I had been meant for Raiden all along. It didn't matter who came first at all.

And why shouldn't it exist? In my brief new life I had seen many creatures that shouldn't be real, and there were no beasts more frightening than fate.

"I miss you too," escaped my lips.

I wouldn't stay silent to save my face.

"I'm not a control freak, I swear. It's just wrong that you are so far away, and you seem to look for trouble more than anyone I have ever met except maybe—" Raiden cut off.

"Who?" I asked.

"I don't want to talk about him," he said coolly.

Conrad, I realized. No one ever wanted to talk about him, and I wondered why he was the black sheep of the family. When his true self shone from below his skin, he was terrifying, but he cleaned up nice. He and Raiden had grown up like brothers, and I wondered what made them hate each other now.

A small pain ticked in my heart, and I wondered if some part of my being already knew the answer.

"How about, I promise I will stay out of trouble if you promise to let me out of your sight as little as possible?"

He raised an eyebrow at me, and I knew that had been close to what he had been thinking as well. "And I thought you were going to be difficult," he joked. "We better go. Our bones may be close to unbreakable, but that won't save us from freezing to death."

He walked around to the passenger's side door and held it open for me. I didn't move.

"Are you iced to the road?" he mused.

"Did you say, unbreakable?"

"Almost unbreakable," he clarified. "We're pretty capable of breaking each other's bones. Please don't test it. Now get in."

I climbed in the Jeep. The engine was off, but the inside was still warm. I hadn't realized I'd been shivering when I was wrapped in Raiden's arms.

"At least I know I won't break my neck falling out of any trees," I mentioned as he slid in the other side. He shot me a look, searching my eyes, daring me not to be kidding.

"I thought we had an agreement. No climbing out of trees."

"That wasn't the agreement. Besides, I'm grounded. If you want to see me outside regular school hours, there is going to be a lot of climbing up and down trees."

He laughed as he kicked the Jeep into gear. I was surprised how little we slid around in the ice. "Who says I don't have a plan for that as well?"

I had no doubt that he could have a plan for everything.

Lena was waiting for us as we slid into

the back row of the parking lot. She had ripped open my door before Raiden had even put the jeep in park.

"Morning, sunshine!" she called to Raiden. "Did you brief her yet?"

"Brief me on what?"

She glared at Raiden with an exasperated expression and pulled me through the parking lot behind her.

"Your ex-boyfriend," she said as if that explained everything.

"What about him?"

"He's a demon," Alex whispered behind us.

FIFTEEN

Tyson was a demon. All the things I had once found attractive about him were now twisted and grotesque. Except for how they had always been, and my human eyes could just never tell.

His skin was completely gray. It was an odd texture too, like snake skin carved of stone. He shouldn't have been able to move.

What few hairs he had looked like black wires and fell to his shoulders. He had no ears, only slits on the side of his hideous face, and he would have been staring right at me—only he didn't have eyes either. Skin covered sockets stood where his gorgeous blue eyes should have been, and he smiled at me.

He knew I could see what he really was, and I was positive he knew what happened to me. He waved before strolling off with a group of girls who wouldn't know better. I even felt bad for them as they snickered at me in plain sight.

I turned and retched in the bushes.

Lena held my hair until I was done. Bile burned my throat in the absence of breakfast I didn't eat.

"You know, skeletons don't really get sick," she said patting my back. "It's all in your head."

"I hope he goes back to Hell," I spat, wiping my hand across my mouth.

I desperately needed mouth wash.

"Hell doesn't exist," Alex said.

"That's negligible," Raiden argued. "But demons don't come from there, they come from people. We think anyway."

My heart stopped. I could feel stomach acid rising back up in my gut.

"That thing used to be human?"

"No, it's a by-product of negative human emotions. Or, I think it is. That or—" Raiden stopped.

He stared at Lena searching for something. Help explaining, or maybe an escape. She just shrugged her shoulders and looked the other way.

"Or what?" I asked.

"Demons are put on this Earth for two things," Alex said from over Raiden's shoulder. "To make man miserable, and to have sex with his wife."

"Huh?" I sputtered, horrified. He couldn't mean—

"What Alex means," Lena explained calmly. "Is that some demons can breed with human women. Tyson, if that is really his name, can create more little creatures of despair just like him. In just nine short months he can have a little clone of his hideous self. It takes humanity years to barf up enough wretchedness to make a demon the old fashioned way. Sex is quicker, and they like it."

The world spun beneath my feet. I

wanted to vomit again but there was nothing left. We had never. I had never—but he had tried. I assumed he was just being a guy.

"Marlow. You didn't know."

Raiden looped an arm around my waist to steady me. It was his scent that helped the most. He sat me down on the sidewalk just as the warning bell rang and I heard Lena groan.

"If I'm late to government again, I'm getting detention," she admitted. "It will be okay! I'll see you at lunch."

She ran, Alex right beside her, his longer legs making the pace easier to keep. Raiden plopped down next me.

"I told you, you were better off without him."

He spoke to the ground, and I remembered. One of the first things he had said to me Saturday in his room was that I was better without Tyson. He had alluded to then, that maybe Tyson was something else. I hadn't even known what I had become then though, so even if he had told me I wouldn't have understood. Not like seeing him here, now.

I stuck my head between my knees just to

breathe. My lungs struggled to fill, I felt like I was being crushed from the inside out. Raiden just sat there, drawing circles on my back, telling me it would be okay.

The tardy bell rang, but we still sat there. I was cold, but the temperature seemed to plunge further as Raiden asked if I had thought I loved the demon.

I hadn't.

"I let him touch me," I admitted. "I let him kiss me. I came so close to—"

I couldn't say it. I didn't want to cry. I wanted to forget.

Raiden's hand had gone stiff between my shoulder blades.

"Can you kill a demon?" I asked.

"With pleasure," he replied.

And I realized he thought I was giving him permission, or that I was asking him to.

"No, I just mean, is it possible?"

How could you kill something that existed from hopelessness? Something created from such negative feelings?

"It is. Despair takes a risk taking a physical form. Although it can never quite pass as human, it can be killed like one, and there are less messy ways."

The school courtyard was empty, and I knew it was only a matter of time before some well-meaning administrator found us. Reluctantly I stood up. I swayed only a minute, Raiden was there. Again he steadied me, and eventually we walked to class, fifteen minutes late.

History was the only class I had with Raiden today and it was torture. It became a test of my will to not stare at him from across the room constantly. Rachelle smirked as she watched my eyes dart from the projector screen to Raiden and back again.

I thought if there was anyone that deserved to have a disgusting demon spawn, it was her. I almost regretted thinking that when the fire alarm went off.

Without fail, the school seemed to pick the coldest, most miserable days of my life to have fire drills. Today surely lived up to those meager expectations, but it did come with a bright spot. I got to spend more non-class-room time with Raiden.

He held my hand as our whole class

walked down the hall in an orderly fashion. I knew something was wrong the moment we saw a crowd outside the double doors of the hall.

The school was on fire. I smelled it before I saw a thing. Then, as we pushed our way through the group of students that stood there aghast, we found huge plumes of smoke coming from directly in front of us. I would have unintentionally joined the reckless spectators if not for Raiden pulling me along.

My legs seemed to trail after him, despite me not remembering to make them move. We eventually made it across the street and to the field that was designed for just this purpose.

Lena and Alex were there.

"Did you see the message?" Alex whispered to Raiden.

"What do you think it means?"

"Who could it be?"

They all spoke at once, and they only seemed to be asking questions. I had no idea what they were talking about. I didn't see any message.

Back across the street, the school didn't

burn, it raged. However, among the roaring flames were places that weren't even singed, and those places made up enormous letters spelling out equally enormous words.

The words read:

SKELETONS OUT OF WATER

Sixteen

Raiden's hand had gone slack in mine. I knew almost nothing of this existence, but one thing I was sure of was that the only skeletons on campus were all standing next to me. Maybe I was wrong.

I could have believed it was the work of a deranged man with a passion for theatrics, if this morning I hadn't found out my ex-boyfriend was a demon of despair. Now I considered what the others were, and that was someone knew our secret. I instantly thought of Tyson. Raiden dismissed the idea right away.

"He wouldn't expose us and risk his own

neck. This is much, much worse than one little demon."

I recalled the sight of Tyson's snake like skin and ears and flinched. Then I thought of the tree beasts I had met in the woods.

Although Alex and Raiden agreed that they couldn't cross them off the list of potential suspects, they also agreed it was unlikely. "They're called Creepers, and they like dark and wooded areas. The odds of them strolling onto our open campus in broad daylight—well, let's just say nothing like that has ever happened before."

I hated to admit it, but I harbored some sort of childish belief that the light would keep me safe, that the dark was where the monsters hid waiting to snatch little girls. It was nice hearing that to some degree that was true. This was January, though, and the winter nights were every bit as endless as the days of summer.

A teacher came to stand beside us as he shouted into his cell phone. He was on the line with 911 dispatch like half the other people at school seemed to be. His presence ended our conversation, but I hadn't been sure I wanted it to continue anyway.

No one went back to class. Half the school was blocked off as a crime scene. Sirens from police cars blared from as far as three counties over. It took half a dozen shiny red fire trucks far too long to put out the flames, and they did nothing to stop rumors from blazing through the student body faster than wildfire.

So far, no one attributed anything to real life skeletons, and I didn't expect that they ever would. Trailers would be brought in while the school was rebuilt. That was going to take days, if not longer.

Raiden didn't say anything as he drove me home in the green Jeep. I still had no answers. I had no desire to question him about anything, because every time I learned something, the world crashed around my head and knocked me to the ground.

Alex and Lena drove behind us in Lena's purple PT Cruiser. It had flames on the side, and pink fuzzy dice dangling from the rear view mirror. The boys parked on the side of the road, and we all got out. Lena was coming home with me.

She and Alex made a big show of saying goodbye, like they had never been apart more than a few hours for most of their lives, and I suspected that was true. Lena was being pinned against the hideous flames on her car, I didn't watch.

Raiden had my face cupped with his hands. They were so warm, and I could feel his pulse in his fingertips. Tilting my head to the side, he bent down to kiss me. His lips brushed mine so softly I worried it might have just been the air. Tickling with the heat of his breath, he pulled away looking at me like he wanted to sling me over his shoulder and never let me go.

"I said I'd keep an eye on you if you stayed out of trouble. Marlow, do not leave the house unless one of us is with you. Something is wrong. Promise you won't leave the house. I'm not being all caveman because I like it."

"I won't leave the house."

"Go," he breathed. "We'll watch you from here."

Lena practically ran down the drive. I struggled to keep up, as I was constantly looking over my shoulder to Raiden, who grew smaller and smaller with every step I took. True to his word, he waited until I could no longer see him before leaving.

We were through the door before Lena seemed to relax at all. Her mouth had been locked in a line for most of the day. My parents weren't home.

"What is happening?" I asked.

"I have no idea," she sighed.

The couch shrieked at our combined weight as we settled ourselves on it. Lena didn't even ask to watch TV. I noticed she had turned on every light in the house on her way to the living room.

"Do bad things often—well, come after us?"

She shook her head. "Like practically never. Sometimes the Creepers get a little over zealous in their plots to control all of the woods. I don't think they did this, and it's been a long time since anything terrible has happened at the lake."

The way she said *terrible* made me realize

she believed in an awfully loose meaning of the word. I had drowned there, and I was almost positive that was where Cassie had killed herself. She hinted we had been close to the same fate, I wondered if our deaths would have been similar.

I shivered, and for the first time I realized how cold the house had gotten, colder than when I had left the window open in the night —almost as cold as outside.

The floor above our heads creaked.

Someone was upstairs. Someone was in my room.

I held my breath and listened to footsteps. The pounding of the intruder's feet echoed through my mind, and I vaguely heard Lena speed dialing someone on her cell phone.

Whoever was upstairs was walking down the hall that leads from my room to the stairs. My heart pounded faster than the prowler could walk. I willed it to shut up; it refused to listen, and pounded faster and faster as the stairs were being traveled down.

Lena whispered only three words into her

phone before hanging up. "I need you," was all she said.

Then she was standing, pulling me off the couch and forcing me into the corner. I found it strange that girlie Lena was trying to protect me, that she seemed determined to save me from whatever monster was lurking just at the foot of the stairs.

I heard the final squeal of the loudest, most worn step, and then I saw him.

He had half a face.

Most of one cheek was strung with thin strings of flesh. Teeth were visible through the gaping holes. One eye was exposed in its socket, and it roamed around until it landed on us. The repulsive strands of skin stretched and sagged as he said, "Hello lovelies."

SEVENTEEN

The voice inside my head was screaming, but I had no idea that I had opened my mouth to let it out until Lena slammed her elbow back into my ribcage. The force shook my teeth and sent aftershocks traveling down my spine. I never looked away from the monster at the foot of the stairs.

He looked nothing like Conrad, whose holes could be covered with clothes and easily forgotten. This thing had holes all over his body. His half a face continued to half a neck, which was striped with the same bits of stirringly flesh. Peeking out from his shirt, I saw that the tops of his shoulders were only bones.

I suspected that what lay behind his thick black gloves was just as disturbing.

"I'm surprised that your boys just left you here. Surely they should be smarter than that. Surely." He watched as my eyes continued to roam his broken body, and he flashed me a slow smile. "We can't all be beautiful."

He rushed to where we huddled, arms reaching out like he planned to grab us. This time a scream rattled my ears and through the room—it wasn't my own.

Even through his gloved hand was wrapped around hers, Lena wailed like his touch was burning. He pulled her up by one arm from the floor where she had been crouched, before ripping her cell phone out of the other hand. It made a grating noise I couldn't place.

He crunched it down to bits, and she never stopped screaming, even as he tossed her to the side. The mangled parts and chips of the phone crunched like bones as he threw them on the floor by her feet.

"We're all the same on the inside, Princess. You of all people should know that, but maybe, maybe your friend here already does."

His normal eye never left Lena as she tried to get her sobs under control, but his exposed eye refocused on me. I was no longer afraid—just pissed off. I was sure he was talking about Conrad, and I had no idea how he knew anything about what I had thought about him. No one should.

"It's not her." Lena spoke from the corner she had pulled herself into. "It's not her! Cassie is dead you idiot!"

"You're lying," he spat.

Both eyes focused back on me now. Then he frowned and his shoulders slouched a little more. I am sure if he knew anything about Cassie, he would know she wasn't me. The lack of bright orange hair should have been a dead giveaway, and if not, the way I cowered in fear and didn't try to kick his ass should have proved it.

"What is your name, my love?" he crooned.

"Marlow," I said, barely above a whisper.

Lena, seizing her chance, flung herself at the window in the living room. She threw it open with a force that rattled the whole house as a burst of cold air shot through space. It was already so cold.

The Hollow grabbed her, flinging her into another wall, and this time she didn't get up. She continued to scream.

"You won't be getting away so easy, princess!" he yelled before facing me again. "Now, what was your name again?"

"Marlow," I said, more confident this time.

"Marlow? I like that. I am terribly sorry we have not had the pleasure of meeting before, Marlow. I'm Lance."

"Nice to meet you, Lance," Alex's voice called from the doorway. "But I'm afraid I'm going to have to kill you now."

I didn't think I'd ever get used to seeing the other skeleton's bones below their skin. Alex was terrifying. I had grown used to Raiden's blue glow, but it did nothing to prepare me for the blood red glow that Alex gave off. It took everything I had to not scream at him.

"Not today, I am afraid," Lance said before shooting out the room and out the front door.

Alex slid back out of the window to chase after him but he stopped. A girl—younger than we were—stood between him and the way that Lance had run off. She had dirty blond hair that fell in her face, and wide scared eyes.

She had been left to distract Alex long enough for Lance to get away. In her eyes, you could see that she knew she had been left to die.

"You can kill me if you want," she said evenly. "You would be doing me a favor really. There are more where he came from and I know you are alone. Let me go and call your friends. Then we both win."

Alex was enraged and shook with anger. I could tell it wasn't directed at this girl, and I could also see he was reluctant to hurt her. She seemed so young. I could tell he weighed his options and decided that she was right. He had been the one that Lena had called, and he must have not told anyone else he was coming because I'm sure Raiden would have come with him.

He just nodded at her.

"Thank you," she said, and she ran.

Lena had gone out the front door and walked around to where Alex stood.

Her shirt was wet with tears, and it had started to snow. They just wrapped their arms around each other, and cried. It was weird watching Alex, as a skeleton or otherwise, cry. It was so intimate; I knew I shouldn't watch though I couldn't look away.

Snowflakes had begun to stick to their hair and shoulders long before either of them pulled away.

Then they came inside. Alex sat the in the kitchen until the effects of the lake water had worn off. His clothes were a mess, as it was a habit of the lake to nearly eat them every time. I had nothing to offer except for Lena. I gave back her t-shirt and yoga pants I had worn home from her house.

I went with her upstairs to change so she didn't have to be alone. It was the first time I had been into my room since Lance had been up here and I gasped when I saw my bed. On my own quilt was yet another message:

SKELETONS DO REGRET

EIGHTEEN

Lena was screaming again. I heard the sound of Alex running up the stairs two at a time before he ripped the door open. He had been looking for a rematch, but what he saw might have been worse. The Hollow in the house had been the one who had burned down the school.

The message on my bed was written in sticks of ivory gum, and I realized morbidly that they were almost the exact same color as real bones. I'd never be able to chew them again.

"Oh, hell," he mumbled under his

breath, obviously coming to the same conclusion I had. "I have to call Raiden back."

He called Raiden. Of course he had.

Alex went downstairs to make a call on the phone, but I couldn't leave Lena. She changed slowly, like she had no clue what she should do with herself now. When she was done we went back downstairs. I turned on HBO without her asking and went about checking the rest of the house for anything that would alarm my parents.

He hadn't broken a thing, and that, combined with the message he had left, lead me to believe that he had never intended to meet us here at all. If I had waited for the bus to take me home, I realized, he likely would have been long gone.

Someone was knocking softly on the door, and I knew without looking it was Raiden. Alex let him in. He had brought extra clothes, and I showed Alex where he could change in the bathroom down the hall. I led Raiden to the kitchen as the sounds of reruns floated through the air. I didn't want to talk in front of her, but I didn't want to take my eyes off her either.

She seemed to be taking things worse than me, and that was a huge surprise. Then again, she had told me just yesterday that it had been a long time since the last terrible thing had happened to the people of the lake. I didn't know what the terrible thing was though, and I didn't have anything to compare the recent events to.

"Are you okay?" Raiden asked me as we sat at the table.

"I'm fine. Will Lena be alright?"

His eyes moved from mine to her shape on the couch, and I realized she had fallen asleep. It was probably for the best.

"She's a tough kid," he assured me. "She'll be fine. It's you I'm worried about. You know nothing of this life, but we have thrust you into it, now when it's even more dangerous than before."

More dangerous. I didn't like the sound of that.

He sighed, and for the first time since being home I noticed the clock. It was late, I had a house full of people, I was supposed to be grounded, and my parents should be home any time.

My head hit the table and I groaned.

"What?" Raiden asked. His voice was filled with more pain than my current thoughts warranted. I liked that he cared so deeply, even if I didn't fully understand it.

"I'm grounded," I reminded him. "And I have three people in my house I am too afraid to be without. What should I do?"

"Cook dinner," he answered.

His response had caught me so off guard, I laughed. Maybe he was just a normal guy after all—always hungry.

"How does that help anything?" I asked.

"In my Jeep—which is, for once, parked in front of your house and not out in the road—you will find all the ingredients needed to make my mother's famous turkey tacos."

"You have a mother?" I asked. He eyed me skeptically. "Of course you have a mother." I wondered why I had ever thought otherwise. If Abraham was a skeleton, someone would have been meant for him.

"So dinner," he continued.

"Okay?" I asked, still not following him.

"Tell your parents that since you're grounded and not allowed to leave, we've come to treat them to dinner. We even brought our own chaperones!"

Maybe Raiden always did have a plan. Either way he was setting himself up for my parents to love him, and I would never be able to make that up to him.

As it turned out turkey tacos were easy, and smelled amazing. I hadn't eaten anything all day. Ground turkey, tomatoes, onions, and peppers sizzled away in my mother's giant skillet.

Alex passed out on the couch next to Lena, curled around her like he was using his body as some kind of shield. I had to be happy with the occasional touch of Raiden's hand on me, or the brush of his body against mine as we moved about the small kitchen.

I heard the sound of our truck pulling into the drive and raced to the living room to get Alex and Lena. They were already awake.

My parents were happy to see Lena again, even if they did occasionally frown at Alex and Raiden. Of course they knew what happened at the school.

"I heard one of the deputies say they

think it was some weird gang activity," Dad said, biting into a turkey taco.

To avoid questions we couldn't answer, we stayed silent on the issue, and I hoped that came off as shock instead of guilt.

"They said they called the FBI," my mom said as she fussed around the kitchen. "Raiden dear, I can't believe you cooked all this by yourself!"

I knew she was thinking my father purposely burned toast just to get out of minimal cooking duties, and was pleased that Raiden had managed to win her over with such little effort.

Of course, she had no idea what was buried under his skin.

Nineteen

When it came time for the night to end, I was in a panic. Even though school had been officially canceled for the rest of the week, I couldn't handle being alone. I looked at Raiden to see if he had a plan, anything that would delay our inevitable separation for even a few more minutes.

He said nothing other than to thank my mother for allowing them over, even though I was grounded. To shock me further, my mother suggested they would relax my grounding even further.

I stared at Raiden harder. He was even better than I could have imagined.

Alex and Lena went out the door, giving us a moment to say goodbye in private. Well, as private as I was going to get with my father gawking at us from the couch.

Raiden wrapped his arms around me. He still smelled like taco seasoning as he leaned in close. At first, I thought he was going to kiss me, and all that work he had done to impress my parents would be for nothing. He just leaned in close though, lips less than an inch from my ear he whispered, "Don't fall out of the tree." Louder, he said, "Goodbye, Marlow," and slid something into my hand.

I didn't look down at it until I answered enough of my parent's questions to earn being able to lock myself into my room. They seemed impressed with all of my new friends. Even if the boys dressed a little—*different*. I knew that if the strange group of Hollows didn't kill me in my sleep, I might be able to have a real relationship with Raiden without having to break my parent's hearts.

When the door clicked closed behind me, I unfolded the paper that Raiden had left. It had a million creases, and contained seven numbers—his phone number. I hadn't even had it before now.

I wanted to call it right away, but did my best to rein in the crazy girlfriend tendencies. I typed it into my phone, saved it to my contacts, and threw my phone on my bed. I swept the gum message that still lay on my bed into the trash bin.

I looked at my phone screen again. *I should send him a message so he has my number,* I rationalized.

Is Lena okay? I asked.

I made myself put my phone down. I could not, would not, wait for it to go off. I glared at it sitting on my nightstand, daring it to try and break my will.

Fortunately, I did not have to wait long. It was already beeping before I sat back down on my bed.

She's fine. Are you?

I thought about it. I wasn't sure I would be okay when I turned out the lights. So far today my school had been half burned to the ground, learned my ex-boyfriend was a demon that wanted to get into my pants, and

I had met a group of Hollows that wanted my bones—or something else.

So little time had passed, yet it seemed like years. Did I feel Cassandra's life getting confused with mine? Would it get worse?

I'm fine now. It was the truth, because every light in my room was still on. *When can I come see you?* I added.

You won't. Someone will come get you. We're in the woods now, making a circle from your house, seeing if we can find them.

I want to help, I sent back immediately

No chance in hell. No girls.

My mouth dropped open. In my mind, I could not imagine Raiden uttering such a sexist thing. My checks felt hot, and my eyes stung. The anger rose up in me faster than it ever had before.

Excuse me? I demanded.

My phone rang. I knew it was him before I answered. I didn't even say hello, I was so afraid I'd choke.

"I didn't want to tell you," he sighed. "Dad thinks they were after you and Lena. Well, not you specifically... just the females."

Something about the way he said females

shocked me. Like we were livestock used for breeding only.

"Raiden? If Skeletons are made by the lake, can they have babies?"

Silence greeted me from the other end of the line. Whatever he had expected, I would say this was not it.

"'Can' and 'should' are not the same thing. Sleep, and I swear I will tell you after your parents are in bed. We have all night."

"Okay."

There seemed like there would never be any real answers. Only more questions.

I knew I would never be able to sleep, but I went through the motions to appease my parents anyway. I took a shower, and changed into my prettiest pajamas. They were not at all functional. The blue silk pants shocked me as I tossed and turned in bed. The black lacy top showed the curves of my breasts nicely.

I didn't remember falling asleep. I had been sitting in the middle of my bed, staring at my old nightlight. I had found it in the bottom drawer of the bathroom and was thankful my father hated to throw things away. The light from my ceiling fan would have been a dead giveaway I was still awake, and I needed them to think I wasn't.

When I woke up I had fallen onto my pillows, and I was hopelessly entangled in my covers. At first, I had no idea what had woke me, but when I glanced at the window, someone was watching me.

Twenty

I swallowed my scream as Alex slid my window open and stepped into my room. I threw my pillow at him.

"What was that for?" he whispered.

"For scaring the crap out of me!" I shot back.

"Sorry."

"Where is Raiden?"

He looked apologetic as he stood there in the light from my star night light. He shifted his weight from one foot to the other, avoiding eye contact.

"He had to go. He'll be back soon."

I flung myself back on the bed. He hadn't

even called, and now he had sent Alex to babysit me. The smell of fresh snow wafted in through the window, where Alex sat on the ledge. I was thankful at least he didn't track in snow.

"He didn't call," I whined.

Alex was frowning. The low light exaggerated the lines of his face making him seem older and graver than he was. He looked like he was made of shadows, but even that wasn't as frightening as he had been when his bones were showing.

"He said you didn't answer."

I grasped blindly for my phone on the nightstand. Sure enough, I had missed a call from him. It blinked letting me know he had left a message.

"Hang on a sec," I told Alex.

"Marlow it's me," Raiden started. "I know I promised you I'd see you tonight and that we would discuss things— but something has come up, and I need to get my mother and Bill. Alex will explain about them. You can ask him anything you wanted to ask me. He said he'd be a good sport. I'm nothing without you, and I'll see you as soon as I can. Don't fall out of the tree."

I wanted to replay the message just so I could hear his voice again. I also didn't want Alex to think I was insane. I threw my phone back at my nightstand and it bounced off, heading for the floor. Alex caught it in one out stretched hand. I hadn't even seen him move.

"First question—do we have super powers?"

"We are good at different things, yes. None of them defy physics. It's more that humans never bother to live up to their full potential."

"We're fast?" I asked.

I had lost sight of Lance in a matter of seconds today. I couldn't be sure if it was him, or a product of the situation and how I had been feeling at the time.

"Some of us are quite fast, yes."

"Can Conrad and Raiden breathe under water?"

He laughed out loud before slapping his hand over his mouth. He must have forgotten that we were supposed to be quiet. I listened for a moment to see if anyone was coming up the stairs, but I doubted my parents could hear. I heard the buzz of the old fan they used to drown out the noise of the rest of the old things in the house. They did not stir.

"Sorry," he apologized. "Your question struck me as odd. I can't believe you went swimming in the lake with Raiden and he never thought to tell you that we don't have to breathe when we're in it."

I stared at him dumbly. I could breathe under water, and no one had ever told me. Well, at least that explained how the boys kept sneaking up on me, and next time I wouldn't be so easy to trick. I asked him not to tell anyone I knew.

He thought that was a great idea. I could tell I was really going to like being friends with Alex, which was nice. I had only been thinking of him as my friend's boyfriend, but I genuinely liked him. Like Raiden said, he was being a very good sport.

When we were sure we weren't about to

be caught by my parents, he pulled my desk chair over to the bed and kicked his feet up.

I thought carefully about what I wanted to ask him next. I knew that Raiden had said I could ask him whatever I wanted to ask him, but I didn't want to completely mortify Alex.

"Alex?"

"Hmm?"

"I hate to ask but..." I paused.

He just raised his eyebrows and leaned in closer.

"Earlier, when I was on the phone with Raiden he implied... well, that we... and by 'we' I mean whatever it is all of us are."

He nodded.

"That we could have kids, but that we shouldn't. I was just wondering why."

Alex took a deep breath. I could tell he didn't want to answer, I could also tell by the new slouch in his shoulders he has resigned himself to it anyway. It was three in the morning, and the world beyond my window was pitch black.

"The thing is, Marlow..." He slumped

down even further. "Okay," he started over. "Raiden and I agree on a lot of things, but we don't agree on this."

"So you think we should?" I asked him. He raised an eyebrow as he pushed the chair onto its back legs, and I blushed. "Um," I stuttered. "I didn't mean *we* like, you and me."

"I know what you meant, Marlow. It's just more complicated than that. It's a purely selfish thing to do, and it's not that I think we should or shouldn't so much as I have already agreed I would."

"You would what?"

"Have kids... with Lena... she made me promise."

I had never seen a guy Alex's age talk about having kids. It would have been sweet if not for the pained expression he wore. "You don't want to," I realized.

"It's not that. If I knew Lena wanted it for just her— I'd give her anything, Marlow. Just like Raiden would give you anything. Anything, except maybe this."

I didn't understand why Raiden would

be so against something that Lena and Alex were okay with. It didn't make any sense.

"If she doesn't want to do it for her, then who does she want to do it for?"

This was the first thing I asked him I was almost positive he wouldn't answer. I was shocked when he did.

"Her mother."

"Her mother?" I repeated.

He nodded. I didn't think it was so strange that someone wanted to be a grandmother. Maybe that was just me.

"She had a baby."

"Lena?" I gasped.

"No!" He threw his arms up, exasperated. "Her mother!"

"Oh. Did it die or something?"

He looked pissed at the whole world, and even more pissed at me for making him talk about what he was mad about. He jerked himself out of chair and started pacing by my bedside. Just like I had seen Raiden do before.

"No, he's just fine," he finally said.

I knew Lena's mother wasn't her biological mother. None of their parents were, but it didn't seem like there were any other children that lived in Lena's house.

"Who is it?" I asked.

"You know who it is," he shot back. I stared blankly back at Alex as he sighed and flopped back into the chair. "It's Conrad."

Twenty-One

"But Conrad is Abraham's son," I said dumbly. "Is Abraham his real father?"Alex nodded slowly. "Oh God! Is that... where Hollows come from?"

He looked away from me then. I had no idea what to think about him and Lena wanting that. I had never given much thought to having children, but I didn't like the idea of the decision being taken from me. At least Raiden and I agreed. I couldn't knowingly do that to a child.

The air in the room suddenly seemed very thick between Alex and me, and in that moment my mind came up with something else.

"Lena's mom—"

"Laurel," he prompted.

"Laurel. She is Conrad's mother."

He nodded. "She isn't the one who raised Raiden." He was standing again, shaking his head. "And that is where the problem is."

"She didn't want to?"

He was trying to decide what to tell me. I could see it in the way he bit his lip and kicked his feet. Poor Alex, it wasn't his fault any more than mine that he had to play teacher to lost little me.

"I love Lena in ways I know you don't understand," he looked up to me. "Just like you love Raiden and if you tried you couldn't explain it. For the rest of us, it built up over time. I didn't just wake up one morning and knew I loved her—but maybe I always knew. You just had it slam into you, every bit of intensity that is in us all. Raiden worries one day you will regret it. That you really didn't have a choice. You know, he loves you."

He loves me. Raiden loves me. It sounded insane, to think I hadn't realized it before. It was something that I had taken for granted. Of course he loved me. The sun rose in the morning and the stars filled the sky at night! Of course.

Here Alex spoke, like none of us had a say in the matter, and I had to decide if I was okay with never having a choice. Who wouldn't choose love?

"The reason we all love each other, the reason we don't have a choice—we're all supposed to be dead. A long time ago, a group of the first Americans came and saw the lake for what it was. Believing it was their duty to protect the energy that gathers there, they offered their lives to it. They lived to the end of their days as mortal men—lonely warriors. The Lake has some level of consciousness, and in its own bizarre way views us like its children. It wants us to be happy. So when those first men began to die off, it took their life force, their soul, and split it in half. It gave half to a new man, and half to a woman."

What Alex had said sounded like the plot of movie I'm sure I would have cried through. I just sat there, picking at the frayed edge of my quilt. I wasn't thinking. I didn't want to.

He was sweating and pacing again. I'm sure he was hoping I'd go back to asking about superpowers.

"Abraham and Laurel, they don't share a...God it sounds ridiculous to say it. They don't share a soul, do they?"

"I know," he sighed. "And no, they don't."

"Then why did they...?"

He just shrugged. I supposed the only people who would know would be them.

My phone beeped, saving us for drawing out further the awkward moment we had found ourselves in.

I'm on my way back.

"Where is he?" I asked Alex.

"Picking his mom up from the airport in Des Moines. Bill is in school there, so he's coming back too."

I wanted to ask Alex a million other questions. Who was Bill? Where had Raiden's mother been? Was she always gone? I had never even seen her, but I remembered the hallway in Raiden's house. I remembered how perfect it had been, far too clean to be maintained by three bachelors for sure.

"Do you have to babysit me all night?" I asked Alex.

"No...unless you are absolutely not okay with him watching you, then I guess I could sleep on the floor or something."

"Who?"

"Conrad. He's already here. Don't worry—you don't have to let him in. He can stay in that tree all night. Can I please go home?"

Alex was looking at me hopefully. I wanted to say no. Hell, I was close to offering him my own bed just so he wouldn't leave. I knew he wanted to see Lena, though, so I agreed as cheerfully as possible.

When Alex left, my room was cold again. My night light didn't seem to give off as much light as before and I felt alone, even though I knew Conrad was just below me. I only dozed, and I awoke often thinking I felt his eyes on me, but whenever I looked he was never there. I had no idea if it was all in my head.

There was one thing I knew for certain: Conrad was nothing like Lance. I thought for sure Conrad had been a monster with his cold laugh and hateful cruel words. I was starting to think those were the defense mechanisms that had gotten him through life. Growing up must have been a nightmare. Having to live so close to his parents when they were meant for other people.

Had he always known?

Lance had been really evil. He could have killed people in the school fire. He snuck into my house and had possibly planned to abduct Lena and I. Where had he come from? If the Hollows were only the children of these Skeletons, then whose child was he? No one seemed to have known him, Lena surely hadn't. I was sure Alex would have mentioned it if he had.

I had so many questions, and below me someone waited who maybe had answers. I walked to my bedroom window and opened it.

Twenty-Two

I waited, but Conrad never came.

Had he left me alone?

I stuck my head out the window and I saw him leaning against the base of the tree. He wore an old hunting jacket, red and black plaid, with a ridiculous matching hat. It was too big for him. Combined with the distance, it made him look small.

Or maybe it was just everything I had learned about him tonight.

The night was darker than I had ever seen. The ground held beautiful fresh snow that managed to glow like it was being fueled by a fire in the center of the world. I didn't even see Conrad's footsteps—somehow he hadn't managed to blemish the perfect scene.

I breathed in the fresh early morning air, it felt wet on my tongue and it burned going down my throat. I coughed. He didn't look up. I was starting to think he had frozen to death there below my window.

With my hand I slapped at the snow on the branch closest to my window. Snow fell from it like a rainbow. There was no wind to push it back into the sky; it only arced with the effort I had used to clear it off. I grabbed my coat and climbed.

I knew he heard me call his name, but he didn't turn around. His shoulders hunched further with every bit down I went. He looked like he was trying to shrink himself into nothing.

When I got to the lowest branch I stopped. Snow continued to fall from the tree around me, but Conrad would not look in my direction. I sat awkwardly on my branch, and just watched his back.

An odd idea struck me.

"Are you mad at me?" I asked.

"I promised my father and brother that I

would not go into your room, and that I wouldn't even climb the tree. I did anyway."

"When?"

"The first time was when Alex was still here. He was talking about me; I figured it was my right."

I nodded my head. If he had been here since we had talked about him, he had heard most of our chat. Maybe he should be angry with me. Even if none of it was my fault, I made both him and Alex relive it.

"When else?"

"On and off the last hour. You kept tossing and turning and—"

And? I wondered. And what?

"You kept saying my name in your sleep."

If I had not had a good hold on my branch I would have fallen out of the tree. My face flamed and I hoped that he couldn't see me blush in the darkness.

He had no malice in his voice, and I had no doubt he was telling the truth. I had been thinking of him before I had fallen asleep. Thinking I didn't really know him at all.

"I'm sorry."

"Don't be," Conrad said. "It gives me hope."

"I love Raiden," I blurted out.

I worried that was more for my benefit than his.

I remembered the first time I had seen him outside the lake. I had thought he was perfect then, and he still looked it. Now when he turned around to face me his eyes held a sadness that wounded me in a way I didn't know was possible. I had no idea what Cassandra had felt for him, but I had to find out. I was almost positive, that was what was killing me now.

"Did you love Cassie?" I asked him mournfully.

It was the question I had longed to ask Raiden, it was the question I had avoided with Alex last night. I knew the answer, but I didn't really want to hear it. I needed to though.

"I loved her soul, I guess." He shrugged. "It's hard to talk about her like she's dead because it's there, in you. It calls to me, you know. Just like it calls to Raiden. It's not fair."

Life is never fair.

"It sings this song, like a Siren leading men to their watery graves. You know that it will kill you, but you follow it just the same, because you can't not."

He kicked the tree, and the rest of the snow fell in waves around me, landing on my head and shoulders. I just sat there wrapped in ice, feeling guilty for something I couldn't change.

I didn't know what I was doing as I climbed the rest of the way out of the tree. He was facing away from me again and I didn't blame him. I wouldn't want to look at me either.

I crossed the space between us in three steps and touched his back tenderly. I needed to say I was sorry. I didn't have the words, and I didn't know what I should be sorry for, but I had to say *something*. I opened my mouth just as he turned around on me.

I stopped moving, but his lips were already on mine. *No,* my mind screamed with every thud of my heart. *No!*

This kiss was different than any I had ever had in my life. It wasn't desperate, but hopeful. He was timid at first, like he expected me to pull away. I should have, but I couldn't, or maybe I just didn't want to. Maybe I was just too weak. His lips were so soft, so careful, and even when he grabbed me and pulled me closer, I was never afraid of him—only myself.

Conrad stroked my hair, and told me he loved me again and again through ragged breaths and too many kisses. I believed him, I didn't want to but I always would.

My body was completely pressed up against him now. I swore I could feel every bit of blood that coursed through his veins. It was so warm. It was making me insane, and I liked it. I hated myself, but I did.

I was too caught up to feel guilt, or even notice that someone else was watching.

The sun began to rise over the trees to the East, blanketing the lower sky in pinks and purples like it was the road to heaven. In a few moments, I would be in hell. When the sun came up, I didn't even watch.

"Don't do this, Conrad," said a quiet voice from behind us.

At first I struggled to place it, then horrified as I realized it was Raiden. He had come back. I was the monster, even if it was Conrad who did not let go. I just stood there limp, still in his arms. Raiden should be mad at me.

He didn't sound angry, just hurt.

"You can't ask me not to try," Conrad said.

He still did not release me. I wasn't sure I wanted him to either, and I hated myself for it.

"I can," Raiden said. "And I will. We all know how it will end."

"Do we?" Conrad smirked, and it was like being stung with a whip. "I doubt it will end exactly the same ever again."

He let go, and the cold that had been so near before overwhelmed me. I stood too close to the two people my soul sung to, to feeling completely alone. I deserved it. I deserved to be alone.

"You didn't even tell her," Raiden said softly.

His sad eyes were on mine, and though his voice bit, they still were not hostile. I wanted him to scream at me. I wanted him to make me promise never to do it again. I would have promised then, but I was so good at breaking them.

"Tell me what?" I asked.

Somewhere in between I had managed to speak, though I had no idea how. If I could form questions I thought I should at least apologize. I couldn't, I needed to and I refused to. Yet another reason I was a beast.

"That he killed Cassie!" Raiden shot.

His eyes darted from mine to Conrad's and they blazed like a spark igniting a wildfire. I flinched, that hatred should have been for me.

If we shared a soul, did that make it physically impossible for Raiden to loathe me like he should? Like I deserved?

"He didn't kill her," I said weakly. "She killed herself, she told me so."

Two sets of eyes turned back to me. I couldn't decipher anything behind them. Pain swirled around me like a cutting wind that stung, and left wounds that felt all too real in their wake. The air was still. It was only in my heart and head.

"What?" Raiden asked, with a voice that

wasn't his own at all. It was both small and loud, like the echo of shattering glass, like the sound of his breaking heart.

"Sometimes she talks to me in my head," I whispered.

Knowing that made me sound insane, knowing that I was insane, standing here, breaking both those boys' hearts over and over.

Why couldn't I stop?

"That's impossible," Conrad sighed.

He looked back at Raiden though. Just to make sure, he wanted him to tell him he was right, that it was impossible.

He couldn't.

"This whole situation is impossible," Raiden said.

He stated walking away. Back to the drive that would lead him down the road where his jeep was parked. Away from me.

"Wait!" I wanted to beg. "Wait!" I should have screamed. But no words came from my open mouth.

"Call me when you know what you want. Obviously it isn't me, not here, not right now."

My voice kicked back in.

"I know what I want!" I cried.

"No," he snapped. "You don't."

Conrad stood silent next to me. He still didn't move. Together we watched Raiden's back as he walked away. I hated that I felt like he was walking out of my life for good. I hate that his footsteps in the snow were soon all that was left of him. I hated that I couldn't make him stay, and I hated even more that he wouldn't just hate me for it.

I didn't speak. I didn't sob. Silent tears raced down my cheeks before they could freeze. I just brushed them off. I climbed the tree to my window. Conrad reached to help me up but I refused to take his hand. I could never touch him again. I was worried what would happen if I did. I was more concerned with ever having to live through what would happen with Raiden if I was too weak.

And I was weak so I did not say a word to him. I did not break, but how I wanted too.

Like the ghost I was, I slunk back to bed. I shed my coat, and even forgot that I was wearing my attractive pajamas. I fell asleep hard. My whole body and mind were exhausted.

When I woke, my room was bright, like sun had exploded into it. When I looked up, Cassie was sitting on the end of my bed.

"I'm still asleep?" I mumbled.

"How should I know?" she asked. "I'm dead."

I pulled the pillow in front of my face.

"This is my fault," she sighed. "You're making all my same mistakes."

I sat up again.

"Do you mean Conrad?" I asked.

"I hate to think of him as a mistake—he was my best friend since I came to Skeleton Lake, and I love him. If I had never strayed, though, my life would have been a lot less complicated. To start, I'd still have it."

I processed what she was saying. She loved Conrad. She said he was her best friend. I imagined them playing together as children. It was creepy to envision child skeletons running on the shores of the lake. I liked the idea of Conrad happy, though.

How had it all happened?

I wanted to ask her, but then I really woke up.

Real sunshine streamed from my bedroom window. I ran to look out but Conrad was no longer there. I didn't blame him either.

I had just sat back on my bed when I heard a knocking on the door downstairs. My body tensed, and my heart raced fast enough to have broken my rib cage, if my bones hadn't been unusually strong. I wondered if the Hollows would have bothered to knock.

TWENTY-THREE

"Marlow!" my mother called from up the stairs.

I held my breath. Maybe Lance would at least spare my parents if I just went quietly.

"Lena and Alex are here to take you away! Hurry and get dressed."

They hadn't left me alone. Even though they should hate me, someone still made sure I was taken care of. That only made me feel guiltier. If I had been dragged deep into the woods by Hollows, I wouldn't have to worry about hurting anyone else.

Though that would hurt them too, at least it would only have been one more time.

I didn't even look at the shirt I pulled over my jeans. I was down the stairs with my shoes flung over my shoulder in less than two minutes. Alex deliberately avoided my eyes. I had no idea if that was because of our conversation last night, or because he had spoken to Raiden. Neither of them was good.

Lena looked infinitely better than they last time I had seen her. She was back to her bubbling self, entwining her body in one of Alex's arms. Her fingers laced in his, as she surveyed his face. Trying to decide what was wrong.

She smiled at me as I hit the last step, but the one I returned with felt fake even to me, like trying to force the frown of a sculpture to smile. The only thing I could force to move of my face were my lips, and I was sure what came of it was more of a snarl.

It was Lena's turn to frown, but at least she didn't say anything.

We bid my parents farewell. They asked us where we were going and Alex gave an answer I neither heard nor cared about.

There was a red car parked in front of my house that I had never seen before, but I immediately knew it belonged to Alex. Its blood red color matched him almost too perfectly. It had two doors, and a black rag top that was thankfully up.

The few birds that remained for winter chirped in the sun. It was so warm the snow had begun to melt, and the sound of running water filled the whole world.

Life went on when I wanted to die—and stay dead.

I got in Alex's car. I hadn't even fastened my seatbelt before Lena had to ask, "What is going on?"

I couldn't see her eyes as she set in front of me, but I knew she was staring at Alex and not me. I didn't know if I should be happy she wanted him to tell her or not.

He didn't say a thing. He just put the car in drive and started on the way to the lake.

"Marlow," she said. "What's wrong? Why isn't either of you saying anything?"

I wondered if Alex would hate me any more if I puked in his back seat.

If we were going back to the lake, then I would have to see Raiden, and maybe

Conrad, and I wasn't sure I could handle seeing either of them.

"Alex... why won't you answer me? Did something *happen* between you guys?"

The way she said happen made me want to vomit all over again. Alex was the only guy I currently wasn't entangled with and I wanted to keep it that way.

"Of course not, Lena," Alex sighed. "It's about Raiden and Conrad." I waited for Lena to judge me, to tell me how stupid I was being. I wanted someone to be angry enough at me to yell. I wanted to yell at myself. She didn't say anything. "He'll forgive you. He doesn't have a choice."

I didn't know which he, he was talking about. I assumed he meant Raiden, as they were usually together. I didn't want him to forgive me; I wanted him to hate me. I especially didn't want him to if he didn't have any choice.

"Marlow? Do you know why Cassie killed herself?"

I shook my head, as I felt Alex let off the accelerator. A wave of conflicting emotions engulfed me as he pulled off the road. In the back of my mind I heard Cassandra sigh. It hurt. All of it hurt.

Alex got out of the car and Lena climbed into the backseat with me. I just started at the headrest; I didn't think I could look at her. Out of the corner of my eye, I saw the blur that was Alex wander into the woods.

"She loved both of them," Lena admitted. "I never understood how she could do it. My heart only exists for Alex."

"It killed her?"

No, that wasn't right. She had killed herself; she was responsible for her situation. Not a product of it.

"She dragged the decision out much longer than she should. Then one day, she found out it had been taken out of her hands."

"What happened?"

"She got pregnant."

My breath hitched. My hands shook. I clamped them down on my knees but that only made my whole body shake. Was that the real reason Raiden didn't want children?

"Raiden's someone's father?"

"She died before the baby was born. She

realized too late what her decision should have been. The baby wasn't Raiden's. He refused to touch her, or even look at her, until she made up her mind. Conrad—well you've met him, his morals leave a lot to be desired. As she grew, Raiden became more distant. You can't slice off half of your soul and expect to live through it. If you hadn't come along when you did, I'm sure we would have lost Raiden, too."

There was little Lena could have said to make me want to live through the kind of emotional devastation I had caused, but this worked. I smiled at her, and this time it was real. I had never been one for close girl-friends. It always seemed like so much effort for nothing, but I was glad Lena was in my life.

"Good!" Lena said climbing back into the front set. "Now where did Alex go?"

"He walked into the woods."

Her eyes scanned the tree line, frowning. She had the door open and was running to the trees before I had even seen what was going on. Alex was fighting with someone—Lance. I ripped my phone from my pocket. I prayed for reception, and that he would pick up.

On the third ring he answered.

"Marlow," Raiden said. "Where are you? Alex said he was bringing you home."

"We were on our way. Alex is fighting with Lance on the side of the road!"

"Are you in the car?" he asked.

"Yes."

"Don't get out. I'll be right there."

I was glad he didn't make me promise. I fought with the seat on my way out the door. Eventually I made it. Then I tumbled to the ground, and I looked up. Standing in front of me was a boy I had never seen before, and both his arms were nothing but bones.

Twenty-Four

He wasn't smiling as he looked down at me. I wish he was the one who was fighting Alex—it looked like it would have been a much fairer fight. It wasn't that Alex was small, exactly. He was tall, but slighter than Conrad and Raiden, and he looked down right puny compared to Lance. He was going to get himself killed.

Lena screamed. I couldn't see what was happening. The boy with the skeleton arms was in my way. Then he reached down and grabbed me by my hair, and I was screaming.

I heard someone yell at him, and he

dropped me. To my surprise, it wasn't Alex or Lena. It was Lance.

"Don't hurt her, stupid!" he spat. "She's mine!"

That was the distraction Alex needed to gain the upper hand. While Lance was busy ordering people around, and pissing me off, Alex got to his feet and landed a solid kick to Lance's mid-section. When he doubled over, Alex punched him in the nose. Blood splattered everywhere, and it looked so much worse in the half melted snow.

The boy that had been blocking my view hurried to aid his friend that was quickly losing the fight. He never got there. A black truck screeched up to Alex's convertible.

We all watched as Raiden and a tall blond ran out of it, and in that moment the Hollows were gone. Lance had dripped a trail of blood into the woods that Alex wanted to follow. He was hurt too though, and Raiden wouldn't go with him.

"We need to get home. We need to get the girls home," Raiden said sternly. "Don't be stubborn."

He just nodded, eyes searching for Lena where she sat in the snow and mud.

"Did that girl hurt you?" he asked her. "I should have killed her yesterday."

I hadn't even realized she had been there. I don't think I would be willing to follow around someone who was willing to just leave me for dead.

"I'm fine," Lena answered. "But you're bleeding. Come on, I'll drive."

Together they stalked off to Alex's car. I heard them speed away, but I didn't get up. I didn't even know how to act around Raiden anymore. He didn't seem to know how to act around me either.

"Ugh," groaned the new guy. "This is worse than I thought. Come on kids, let's get you home."

Raiden scoffed at the word "kid." I felt the same. This guy was maybe a few years older than we were.

I ended up sitting center seat with them in the truck. When we were on the road again the driver turned to me and said, "I'm Bill, by the way."

"Marlow," I said miserably. I would have rather been anyone else at all.

"Yes," Bill said. "I've heard a lot about you."

I was sure it was all terrible, so I didn't ask.

When we made it to Raiden's house, it was a nightmare. There were so many people there I had never met, and they all looked at me with pity or disgust. I hated that the first time I met Alex's parents they were busy fussing over his wounds, which were partially my fault.

If we hadn't stopped there, he wouldn't have gotten hurt. I was tearing these people apart. I was ruining their lives.

"This isn't your fault," Conrad said behind me.

Raiden had wandered away the moment we walked through the door.

"It *is* my fault," I countered. "And don't take this the wrong way, but I can't be around you right now. I might not ever be able to be around you. I know now isn't the time for it, so please just leave me alone."

He didn't say anything after that, and

Lena scooted over on the couch to make room for me next to her. She had enough to worry about right now, but she wrapped one arm around me anyway.

"It will get easier," she said.

I wasn't sure I believed her.

Lance had bit Alex in at least three places, which just showed what a creepy bastard he was. Alex's mother, who I was still shocked to see was of Asian descent (even knowing all the kids here were adopted), was busy cleaning all the teeth marks with something smelly and purple. I turned up my nose, but he didn't seem to mind.

When they pulled off his shirt to inspect his chest for further injuries, I politely excused myself. I found myself wandering the hallway that lead to Raiden's room, and I was surprised to see someone else there.

She was a small woman, with her graying hair up in a bun. She looked like she hadn't slept in weeks, but she was still beautiful.

"You must be Marlow," she said.

Her voice was even and she looked like she was working very hard at it.

"Yes."

"I'm Melissa, Raiden's mother."

I just stared down the hall at her. She hadn't come any closer, and I hadn't gone any closer to her. I was sure if I did that she might try and rip my throat out. She ground her teeth like she might.

"Why do you insist on hurting my son?"

"It won't happen again."

She laughed at me. It was cold, and the many lines on her face stood out.

"You can't promise that. I am curious though, why you think you won't?"

I stared at her, and I hated that she was right. I couldn't promise that I would never hurt him again. I could promise that I would try, and I had made my decision. I told her as much.

"Because I've heard that before," she said bitterly.

And I remembered that this was a woman who had been cheated on before.

"I'm sorry," I whispered.

"I should hope you are," she mumbled as she walked past me.

Raiden's room was just down the hall, and I noticed his door was open now. He stood in the doorway. Arms holding him up as he stared at me in the hall.

"Have you really?" he asked me quietly.

"Have I what?"

"Made up your mind?"

Twenty-Five

"Yes," without a doubt.

"And?" he pressed.

"And what? I can't lose half of my soul. Raiden, I can't lose you."

I could barely stand losing you for a few hours, I wanted to add, but he was moving out of the way. He was letting me into his room. Nothing else mattered.

The door hadn't even closed before I had pressed my head into the crook of his neck. I cried, and watched as my tears ran down his shirt, then I realized they weren't just my own. I made myself catch my breath before pressing my lips to his. They were salty.

He moaned into my mouth, and I lost it.

I had been so close to losing this forever. My mind and body went into overload. I couldn't think. I could just go by instinct. I knew what he liked, I knew what I liked. What I craved.

My hands were clasped so tight around his neck I couldn't believe I wasn't choking him. He didn't stop. He held onto my arms like I was trying to run away, but I was trying to press myself further into his body instead.

He sighed and picked me up like I was nothing. I was falling into his bed before I realized the feeling wasn't just caused from an emotional high.

His bed smelled just like I remembered, but his scent above me was even better. His taste was addicting, and I never wanted to recover from it. He licked into my mouth like he expected me to object. I welcomed it. I didn't think I would ever be close enough to him.

Raiden peeled off my shirt effortlessly with one hand. I didn't see where it landed, I didn't care. I only cared his lips were away from my mine. I leaned up to try and capture them—there was a knock on the door.

We froze.

"Son," Abraham called. "You need to come downstairs, we're having a meeting."

"Right now?" Raiden asked.

I did my best to silence my breathing. Abraham had offered us a lot of freedom, but I wasn't sure it would stretch this far and I didn't want to find out.

"Afraid so," was all he said.

Raiden pressed his face into the mattress and groaned. I knew exactly how he felt.

"We'll finish this later," he promised before retrieving my shirt from the floor.

We waited until my breath didn't sound like I had run a marathon in his bedroom before stepping out into the hall. Conrad was standing at the other end of it, arms across his chest, eyes cold. I told myself I didn't care.

I was lying, but it didn't matter. It couldn't matter, because I had made my decision.

He wouldn't move out of the way, we had to squeeze around him to get down the stairs. His eyes followed me the whole time. I just let Raiden pull me along. After a few minutes I heard Conrad trail us to the first floor.

Too many people were crammed into Raiden's living room. Alex stood up so I could sit next to Lena on the love seat. Raiden and Conrad stood by Abraham at the front of the room.

"As you all know," Abraham spoke to the room, "something is wrong. A group of Hollows has descended upon our territory. We don't know who they are, or where they come from. All we know is that they seem to be after our young girls. This cannot be tolerated."

"How many are there?" Laurel asked.

"We're not sure," Raiden answered. "At least fifteen, maybe more than twenty."

I had only seen three of them so far—Lance and the girl, and a new boy today. That was a long way from fifteen.

"One small group of them seems to be stalking Marlow and Lena. They have been to Marlow's home, and they attacked them on the road on the way here," Abraham continued.

I am just happy he didn't go into details

of why we were on the side of the road. That wasn't really important to what we were talking about now.

No one knew what to do. Lots of people spoke, no one offered any answers. They all seemed to think I should stay around the lake. I had no idea how that would work. My parents might let me sleep over at Lena's for a night, probably not for the rest of my life.

They also decided that Bill should go back to Iowa State and get the other kids that were there. Apparently, there was a whole other group of kids I hadn't even met yet.

After the meeting was over, Bill and Abraham put their heads together and tried to come up with a game plan. All the different variations of the plan seemed to involve me not leaving the house, so I snuck out early. Raiden had to stay behind to help, but Alex, Lena, and I walked out on the dock.

The sun was setting now, filling the lake with brilliant reds and violets. Somehow it seemed like I had missed a whole day of my life.

"Are you okay?" I asked Alex.

"Oh yeah," he mumbled. "I'm fine."

"Thanks for saving us," I said.

He wasn't looking at me, however. He was standing on the edge of the dock, looking at Lena. Her white hair looked pink in the twilight. She ran her fingers across his jaw, and stood on her tippy toes to kiss his mouth but she stopped, and shoved him hard.

Alex hit the water back first with a splash. Water flew through the air spattering Lena and I. Coloring our skin with dots and dots, where you could see our bones. Lena's were a silvery color that somehow suited her so well. I got a good long look at them after Alex sprung from the water and pulled her in by both legs.

They invited me in and I made Alex turn so I could shed my clothes. They were all I had with me and I didn't want them eaten. He just laughed and did as he was told. I ran off the dock and plunged into the water. It was just as warm as I remembered, and I was glad that at least for a little bit, it let me forget.

Twenty-Six

While swimming in the lake, I didn't notice the shadow lurking just out of sight. It hovered against the side of the house, watching me with pain-filled eyes, before turning his back on us and sliding into the woods.

Out of sight, out of mind.

He was too far away for us to hear his quick steps as he crunched through the slush by the end of the forest. After it was too late, I looked back in that direction, I swore I had felt something go. I just had no idea what it was.

Raiden joined us after I had given up on

trying to trick myself into not breathing under water. I lay flat out on the dock, coughing up lake water and panting in between laughs. Lena and Alex thought I was hilarious, and were laughing even harder than I was.

My ribs ached, and I hoped it was the laughter and not that I had nearly drowned again. The smell of the murky water was all over as Raiden walked down the dock and stared down at me. He was smiling at me as I lay there, his face to me upside down.

"Great news. Laurel has you spending the night at their house for days."

I wasn't surprised. That was almost exactly how I thought it would play out.

"Do I at least get to go back for clothes and stuff?" I whined.

"Yep. Dad's organizing the SWAT team to get you there as we speak."

Great. I needed a SWAT team.

"I hope you're kidding, but I'm sure you aren't. Why can't you take me?"

His eyes twinkled, like he was thinking something I wasn't privy too.

"It's probably best that they not think

you will be sleeping anywhere near me," he shrugged. "Even if you are."

I smiled back. Sounded like a plan to me.

Looking down at my bronze bones, I sighed. It was going to take me forever to get dry. Raiden called Alex out of the water. He and Lena were going to my house. I watched as they streaked back up the hill to where Raiden's house sat and blasted each other with the hose.

At first I had no idea what they were thinking. Now that the sun had set, the air away from the lake was freezing. I couldn't imagine how the outside tap water felt. It was so warm on the dock that I didn't want to move. Before my eyes, Alex and Lena's bones vanished.

"Wait?" I asked Raiden who still stood next to me. "You can wash the lake water off? You don't just have to wait and get dry?"

No one ever shared with me the really important things. That was probably because no one realized I didn't know, and it was really making my whole life more difficult.

I tossed my clothes that had been in a pile on the far end of the dock to Raiden and ran after Lena. I was still several feet away when Alex turned the hose on me. He was completely nude, I noticed, before he blasted me in the face.

"Alex!" Lena chided him. She, too, was naked.

So was I, I realized when I looked down. I was also freezing.

Raiden slipped a towel around me before I had time to be too self-conscious. I smiled back at him.

"Thanks," I whispered.

"No problem."

He bent down to kiss me, and I felt warmer having his body so close to mine. That didn't mean I was.

"Your lips are blue," he mused after a quick peck.

Far, far too quick of a kiss.

"I'll live," I assured him.

"I'm sure you will," he agreed. "But all the same, I'd like to get you inside."

My teeth started chattering, and I knew fighting him on this was a lost cause. I let him carry me inside. I felt light as he walked me inside the door, then heavy as he set me down in front of a room that was not his.

I pouted, and he kissed me. Harder this time, more—just more. I couldn't explain it, like he thought I was leaving for good and never coming back, when really I just needed to pack my overnight bag.

As it turned out, the mystery room was the bathroom. I put my clothes back on and surveyed the damage. I looked the best I had in days. I got the feeling the lake could heal us, and my suspicions were confirmed when I saw Alex. The lake had fixed almost all the wounds he had gotten in the fight with Lance.

"It can't do everything," he explained. "But it can heal the small things, no problem."

That was definitely a good thing to know. I was glad I found it out before I needed to use that knowledge.

Laurel had a purple minivan to go with Lena's purple PT Cruiser. She smiled at Alex as he slid into the front seat next to her, and Lena and I climbed all the way to the back row.

Alex's mom came with us too, and chatted with Laurel as we started down the road. I wasn't sure how a van full of women was going to keep me safe, but apparently they were the only people Abraham could round up.

I was a little surprised he hadn't come himself, but something had happened right before we left. Either it was nothing, or they didn't want to let me know as they rushed us out in a hurry. I was almost positive it was the former, I'd wait and hopefully Raiden would tell me later. I was still sad he couldn't come. I wanted to climb back into his arms and hear whatever it was no one else wanted to tell me.

I stared out the window and into the woods as we drove past. It was too dark to see anything, and I kept my eyes peeled just in case. I didn't know if it was the blackness, or the whole situation, but I felt uneasy. I had seen Alex fight, and I knew he could hold his own, but I also knew who he'd protect if he had to choose. I was positive I was his last priority here.

Lena sat with her arm pressed up against mine. I noticed she was staring out the window too. I leaned closer to her and said, "Something is going on, isn't it?"

She waited for a second to see if anyone had overheard—they all seemed to be engaged in a different, more cheerful conversation.

"It's Conrad," she whispered. "He's run off."

Twenty-Seven

No matter how many times I told myself I wasn't worried, it was still a lie. Lena held my hand—she knew I was upset. She was reluctant to discuss it further and I didn't blame her. After all, Raiden was her friend, and I got the feeling she believed in strictly monogamous relationships.

As we pulled into my drive she pressed her mouth to my ear.

"It's not the first time. It's probably nothing. He needed to blow off some steam. It happens. Mom's not worried."

I knew she was telling the truth. I also knew she was, just like everyone else, keeping something from me. It was my fault he had run off, but I couldn't continue down the same path that Cassie had, and he knew that just as much as I did. It had ended badly before, it would end badly again. Just like Lena said, you couldn't live with only half a soul.

Dad had gone bowling with a few of his friends at work. Mother ended up loving Laurel and Alex's mom, Amy. They talked together for far too long to make me happy. I finally walked upstairs to pack my bag while Lena kept Alex company among the many women.

Alex was a brave guy. He didn't flinch in a fight with a Hollow twice his size, and he didn't bat an eye at a kitchen full of middle aged women.

I walked into my dark room slowly. I was relieved to see there were no cryptic messages on my bed, but I couldn't recall having left my window open. There it was though, curtain blowing in the wind. I frowned as two arms locked around me.

I didn't scream. I wanted to, but I couldn't because my mother couldn't know.

Silently wiggling and kicking I fought and fought the arms around me. They did not budge.

"I knew you would come back," a familiar voice said.

Conrad! My mind screamed. I had been so worried about him, so guilt-laden about his disappearance when he was here in my room all along. I was pissed.

He released me and I slapped him. He didn't even flinch, and that just pissed me off more. I advanced on him further, hoping to focus all my anger on achieving more damage.

Instead, he kissed me. I hadn't even realized his plan until it had already gone on for far too long. This kiss was different than before. This *was* desperation. This was a last chance, and I could taste it, feel it, and I had no idea what to do with it.

I had no idea how to stop it without destroying him, without destroying me. I didn't think it was possible. We tumbled back onto my bed. If the women downstairs could hear us, I knew they'd wonder what was going on.

I still couldn't stop. I felt like I was falling into my mattress under the weight of him, and I thought that might be a suitable end.

He moved his lips to my neck. I still couldn't breathe. I wondered if I ever could again. Conrad didn't stop kissing me to wiggle off my jeans. I let him. Some part of my mind was screaming—the other part of me was dying of anticipation.

His shirt and pants joined with mine on the floor, and then he unhooked my bra under my shirt. His rough hands had just brushed the exposed skin of my breast when my bedroom door opened with a bang.

Alex glared at us from the doorway. He called over his shoulder in a horrible false pretense and said, "Oops wrong door!" It was for the benefit of my mother and no one else.

He walked in and slammed the door behind him.

"Get dressed," he hissed. "I swear I should kill you both right here in this room. You are so lucky my mother is downstairs!"

I was crying. I tried to rein it in, but I was failing. I knew this would happen if I touched Conrad again, and I was forcing myself to not touch him. I had no idea how to force him not to touch me. I was so weak.

"Don't be mad at her," Conrad protested. "She told me not to touch her, but I snuck into her room anyway. Our history is in her, she has no choice!"

"Why are you such an idiot?" Alex wondered out loud, and I wondered which of us he was talking to. "Do you *have* to do the same things over and over?"

"You can't judge me!" Conrad spat in Alex's face. "You have no idea what it's like to be me!"

Alex threw his hands up in the air in clear defeat.

"I'm trying, okay?"

He spoke so softly, I was taken completely off guard by the tenderness of it, the kindness of his eyes. He cared for him. I was amazed I had missed it for so long.

"You're my friend too," he added.

"You could have fooled me Alex! You're always taking his side in everything."

I knew he was talking about Raiden, and just the thought of his blue eyes brought me closer to tears.

"He lost half his soul."

"And now he can have it back!"

Conrad flew open my window and climbed down my tree. I couldn't believe how much his words stung. It was better this way. I couldn't tell, with my vision blurred and Alex still staring at the space that Conrad occupied, but it was.

We were in my room for far too long to not look suspicious.

"Come on, pack. Let's go," Alex said bitterly.

"Are you going to tell Raiden?"

He stared at me so hard I had to look away.

"I should, but it won't help anything."

He ran out of my room. I wanted to go after him. I almost wanted to tell him thanks —I would have if it wouldn't have been completely inappropriate to say.

Throwing things into my bag without looking at them I looked at the window. I had no idea where Conrad had gone now, and I shouldn't care. But I did.

Twenty-Eight

The drive back to the lake was far worse than the drive away. Alex said nothing, and everyone in the van commented on it. He just shrugged them off. I noticed him staring at me in the visor mirror like he was afraid to take his eyes off me. I didn't blame him.

We made it back without incident. I almost hoped for the biggest, scariest Hollow I had ever seen to stroll into the middle of the road looking for a fight.

Almost.

There was nothing but silence, darkness, and the overwhelming shadow of guilt that haunted me more than any ghost ever could.

The houses around the lake were quiet. The few lights that showed through windows spilled onto the water of the lake like eerie beacons.

Alex might not tell Raiden, but I knew I had to. I wouldn't be able to live that lie the rest of my life. I knew I would eventually crack, and I knew I shouldn't wait until I did.

I bid farewell to the others and started on the worn path to Raiden's house. The lake easily warmed the air around it but I shook. I didn't think of what to say. Excuses would shrivel on my tongue like instant death, and the truth was horrible enough without my butchering words.

I just walked until the air grew colder as I approached the house.

When I got there I stood by the front door for far too long as I prayed his mother wasn't home. She was right about me. After what may as well been years, I knocked.

No one answered and I waited with trembling hands and feet. It took so much for me to get there; I didn't think I had enough strength to walk back. My heart was still heavy—I guess it always would be.

Leaning against the cold glass on the door, I sighed. Maybe I would just sleep here until someone came back.

"Marlow? Are you okay?"

Or maybe I'd just die right now instead.

"I'm not okay," I said without turning around. "I'm a monster."

"You aren't a monster."

"You don't know what I've done, or you wouldn't say that."

I waited for him to ask, and I was dreading it, and begging for it at the same time. Just let it end, I mentally pleaded. He said nothing. Perhaps he was drawing his own conclusions. Perhaps that was worse.

It could hardly be better.

"How do you know, I don't know?" he asked. "How do you know Conrad didn't come straight back here, tell me exactly what he did and did not do with you, and asked me to piss off?"

"He asked you to piss off?" was all I could say.

"I'm afraid so. Walk with me?"

If Raiden had asked me to throw myself into the lake and never come back up I would have willingly done it. A little thing like a walk should have been a no brainer. Despite the fact that his voice was smooth, calm, and showing not the slightest hint of malice, I was reluctant.

I wasn't ready for it to end.

I started with him anyway, away from his and Lena's house, to the side of the lake I had never been to. At first, he said nothing. He just slowly went along. He was close enough to touch, but I didn't reach out. I didn't dare.

Finally he stopped.

"I forgive you," he whispered.

"You shouldn't," I admitted.

"I know. It wasn't your fault."

Raiden started walking again and I followed him. I felt numb. I knew I was hurting him. Why wouldn't he hate me like I hated myself?

I clung to the fact, that it might be impossible to hate me. Was that any life to live? Miserable with me, miserable without me. Miserable, untrusted and unloved. A lovely existence it wouldn't be for sure.

Where there were no houses to light the

way, the water of the lake was dark. In one such place Raiden slid down into the muddy shore. He pulled off his pants and waded into the water up to his knees. His blue light was back, and it was even more beautiful. Every time I saw it, it seemed brighter than I remembered. My mind would never do it justice, even when it used to haunt my dreams I had it wrong. I had everything wrong.

The little waves slapped against his legs in a constant rhythm, like breathing that was a little off. I watched his chest expand and contract and I longed to touch him. Even though he forgave me, I wasn't ready to forgive myself.

When I followed him into the depths, I had no idea what I was setting myself up for. I was hopeful. I peeled off my sweater and jeans and deposited them on the shore. I ran into the water, splashing loudly, not caring if I woke everyone around the lake. Hoping I did, wanting them to see us together.

Raiden grabbed my wrist and pulled me to him. I didn't know if he wanted to kiss me, or shake some sense in to me. I would have agreed to either.

Instead, he just pressed his hot cheek to mine, and rocked me in his arms like we were dancing. Round and round in slow circles and swirling splashing waves below our feet, we danced. Clumsy wet steps joined with clumsy wet kisses. We were close together and so far apart. No matter how much closer I managed to get my body to his, it would never be enough.

In the middle of our eerie Macabre of bones and broken hearts, he whispered, "I need to be enough."

We danced all alone on a floor of moving glass. A ball below the canopy of light, the stars were bright, and even the water wasn't as warm as his brilliant bones. He would always be enough, so long as he never let go.

Twenty-Nine

When I woke up, the stars still stretched out above us. Cool grass had been crunched beneath our backs, and Raiden was still pressed up against me. He hadn't slept as I lay there engulfed in nightmares.

I knew I hadn't said Conrad's name in my sleep because I only dreamed of Raiden. Safe in his arms, and content even without pleasure that he had still withheld from me in real life.

Rolling over to meet his lips again, I sighed. I was content, even if the night hadn't gone as far as I would have liked. I understood his apprehension. I shook off the bad dreams. They weren't real. His lips were.

Raiden kissed me back, more sure of himself than he had been last night, and I relished in it. If I could put everything in the past behind me, I knew I could be happy with him. That he was enough. That he always had been.

There was a hole in Raiden's heart. It might not be visible to the naked eye like Conrad's was, but it was there just the same. A huge gaping wound from being ripped apart time and again. I wasn't sure if that hole was ever something I could fill, if I was meant to fill it up, or just be a bandage.

I wished the lake had a voice so I could ask. A human voice, I should say, with human thoughts. It did have its own song, and right now it was beautiful.

Dozing off again, I was concerned I had fallen into another nightmare. Someone was screaming.

I bolted upright, but Raiden was already on his feet dragging me up. Other people were running on the other side of the lake, more women were screaming. I recognized one of the loudest screamers was Lena, I could hear her sobbing in between shrieking.

There was only one voice that wailed above my friends, and I was almost positive that was her mothers. She sounded like she was being killed in cold blood in front of everyone else at the lake.

They all seemed to be out near the water, and in a moment the splashing sound of people running in exploded with a burst of light. Skeletons plunged into the lake. One of them I knew was Alex, but I didn't recognize the glow of the others.

It looked like they were carrying something dark and motionless between them.

"Oh no," Raiden breathed.

He was running, and I knew he wasn't waiting for me to catch up. It seemed too far away from where the others were. I had no idea what time it was, the only thing I knew was that the lake was still dark. Why had we walked so far away from everything last night?

I cursed myself as I tried to push harder. I wanted to go faster and was starting to wonder if it might have been faster if I had just swam.

Raiden was already there, already waist deep in the water next to Alex.

"Was he breathing?" I heard him shout.

Was who breathing?

Then I stopped. I realized what that dark thing in the water had been. It was Conrad, and he hadn't been moving. Raiden didn't even know if he was breathing.

I started to run again. I couldn't feel my legs pounding beneath me. I couldn't feel anything below my heart and bruising lungs.

It was hard to tell how bad of shape Conrad was in just by looking at his lifeless form in the lake. In the water, he had always been particularly grotesque. He had pieces still missing in his middle, but I couldn't decide if it was worse, or all in my head. His bones still seemed to suck the little light out of the air, and I hope that was a good sign.

Laurel was in hysterics, and Lena was doing her best to hold her back at the edge of the water. Then Laurel locked eyes on me, and Lena didn't have a chance. She shook free of her adoptive daughter's embrace and headed right toward me. I had to slam on the breaks to avoid slamming into her.

"You! This is your fault!"

"Mom!" Lena shouted. "Stop it!"

"You stop it!" Laurel shot back.

Lena had wrapped her arms around her mother again, but I wished she would just let her go. I was happy someone was mad at me. Everyone else seemed to ignore that since I had shown up I had done almost everything I could to wreck their lives.

"It is my fault."

"Marlow! It is not. She's just upset. She knows it isn't your fault."

"It is, though! I can't love him, and he ran off and got hurt."

Tears dripped from my chin like a cold rain. They didn't even seem as warm as the air around them.

"Oh God!" Lena sighed. "He was in the woods blowing off steam and he went and picked a fight with the other Hollows. So since they are here trying to run off with all the chicks it just might be my fault as well as yours. Mostly, it's his own stupid fault for being such a dumb ass!"

I heard the sound of Laurel's palm colliding with Lena's face seconds before I realized she had slapped her. I hadn't seen Alex get out of the water at all. There he stood, red skeleton bones, and a face that made him even more terrifying. He had Laurel's arm in his hand of bare bones, dripping water onto her, making her light up as well.

"Do not touch her," he growled. "Conrad is going to live, but you aren't helping anyone. It isn't Marlow's fault he was an idiot. She has no control over her soul. You should know that better than anyone."

He threw her to the ground, but Lena had wrapped her arms around his neck and was sobbing. His skin was resuming its normal flesh tone where her wet tears had run. Laurel sat there staring at her hand in shock. It took Bill coming to lead her away, and into Abraham's house where they had moved Conrad.

I could hear his laughter wafting out the open windows of the lake the house. Alex was carrying Lena away, and everyone but Raiden left me alone to wonder.

"Was this my fault?" I asked him.

He shook his head slowly, his eyes looking back at his, not at me.

"Would you tell me if it was?"

"Probably not," he answered honestly.

Thirty

That night Lena and I slept on Alex's couch. We lay together and talked until neither of us could see straight. Raiden wouldn't let me stay with him because Conrad was there. Even though he didn't believe it was our fault, I knew he felt just as guilty about what had happened to his brother. They had grown up together, loved each other for years; it hadn't always been so tense.

Raiden didn't want him dead. He just didn't want him to love me.

He didn't want me to love Conrad more.

Alex wouldn't let Lena go home, even though no one was there. Laurel did not leave Conrad's side, which I heard pleased Raiden's mother, Melissa, to the point of throwing china.

All in all, it left very few places we were welcome, so we had ended up here. Alex's parents' house was the Japanese one I had seen on my first walk around the lake. It had a full garden according to Lena. I could see another snow storm blowing in just outside the magical arm of the lake, but it didn't even get one flake on the house.

In my mind, I would have thought Alex's mom would have been a very soft spoken Japanese woman, the kind you see in the movies. Amy was a lot different than I thought. She seemed to delight in ordering Alex's father Leo about, and he was equally delighted to do her bidding.

Leo was an insurance salesman, and I found the idea borderline hilarious. No one else did, so I chewed the inside of my cheek to keep from laughing. Really, I needed sleep, but it wouldn't come. Not with Conrad in pain two houses away. Not with Raiden at home dodging dishes. Not with Alex being banished to his own room. Apparently his parents weren't nearly as lenient as Abraham was.

Since I couldn't sleep, I asked Lena questions. In the beginning she wouldn't talk about her mother at all. I understood, they weren't on the best of terms currently, but at some point she decided she would rather get it all out then let it stew inside.

She talked about growing up with her mother, who really just wanted her son back. I had no idea what she meant, so then she had to back track.

Laurel and Abraham had an affair, and everyone knew it before Conrad had come into the picture.

"How does that work?" I asked.

Because the way I understood it was, you got your soul mate, then there was the happily ever after. Bad things didn't happen before I showed up.

I could feel her roll over to gawk at me on the couch.

"How should I know?" she blurted out sarcastically. "I've only ever loved Alex. Maybe I should be asking you."

Oh.

I realized she was right. I had attributed the issue with Conrad as being a one-off, because there wasn't anyone to love, because he shouldn't be. I had attributed it to me being just as broken as he was.

"Why do they call you Laura at school instead of Lena?" I asked, changing the subject.

"That's an easy one," she replied. "My real name is Lena. Most of the others had their name changed when they came to the lake but Mom didn't want to change mine, even though my father begged her to. I have to go by something else just in case someone realizes I'm a missing little girl from so many years ago."

"So," I said. "Tell me about your dad."

That launched Lena into a talk about how awesome her father was. Even though he couldn't be around that often, he loved her, and he even loved Alex, and he loved everyone but Laurel it seemed, I got that.

"How long?"

"Huh?" she asked.

"How long did they carry on this crazy affair?"

She sucked in a jagged breath and groaned. "It sucks having to say these things out loud because everyone knows, but... they still meet. Every week."

That explained so much, I couldn't begin to respond to it. Everything about how Raiden treated me, had treated Cassie, suddenly made too much sense. I was furious I hadn't managed to connect it all before. He saw everyday what it was like to be on the wrong side of love. He knew what it was like to lose, and I could tell he refused to live his life that way.

I wouldn't make him.

"Lena," I nudged her. "Lena, do you think anyone will care if I sneak out of here? Lena?"

She was already asleep.

The couch bed squealed when I got up despite my best efforts to be quiet. I sat perfectly still to see if I had been caught.

"Lena?" Alex called from the hallway.

"It's just me," I assured him. "I have to see Raiden."

"Carry on," he joked before walking back to his room.

Silently, I pulled Lena's sweater over my tank top and pajama bottoms. I knew I wouldn't freeze with the lake so near. I still felt underdressed without my bra, and I didn't want to have to hunt for it in my bag in the dark.

The only light on in the house was the one downstairs, where I knew Conrad was. I prayed he was asleep as I headed for the screen door.

Then I heard voices.

Ducking down below the window, I held my breath.

"Why are you always such an idiot?" Raiden asked.

"Why do you always get the girl?" Conrad countered.

I thought about turning around and sprinting the yards back to Alex's house. I knew I should, but my curiosity was winning out, and I slid down to sit on the wood porch.

Lamp light bled out into a patch in front of me, so I crouched in the darkness. In the smell of wood and dirt that did nothing for my nerves.

"As I recall, that's not true," Raiden sighed.

"Oh please." I could tell Conrad was tired, and in pain. His voice sounded small, even his laugh now lacked a lot of its usual zeal. "You know she loved you more. You just wouldn't give her what she wanted."

"She was fifteen! She didn't know what she wanted!" Raiden shouted.

Through the window I could hear his voice quiver. I wanted too much to hold him, to caress his face and tell him it would be okay, but he couldn't know I was here.

"I know," Conrad admitted. "I also know, the only reason she loved me at all was because the baby tied us together. I know before that, it was only you. There was no room in her heart for me. She used me for one thing, and I let her, even though I knew."

Raiden only responded with silence, but I knew none of that was true.

"I don't know how it works. You've seen it firsthand just like I have. Mom and Dad couldn't quit each other either, even though I knew they wanted to. Maybe if I did die they would be free, but as I am regrettably still alive, despite my best efforts, I am the glue that holds them reluctantly together."

"That doesn't make any sense, Conrad! If Cassie only loved you because she let you knock her up, that doesn't explain Marlow at all."

"She gave Marlow her life force; how it was the day she died. What if she gave her *all* of it?"

Thirty-One

If I vomited on the porch, they would know I had been eavesdropping. I whimpered. Death, skeletons, and half souls in half broken boys was my last thought before I passed out. There was only so much I could take, and I'd been reaching the breaking point since day one.

Coming to, I instantly realized I was being jerked around, manhandled as I was carried up the stairs. Raiden was trying to hold me still, but the stairway was narrow and we bumped and slid along. It was like being on a ship, bound for sea sickness.

"Put me down!" I demanded.

"No, you need to lie down."

"I'm going to be sick, put me down!"

Those were the magic words it seemed. He nearly dropped me at the top of the stairs, where I retched. I felt bad about getting puke on the pristine floor in the hallway, but my head and heart felt worse.

I could hear Melissa *tsk*ing at me from a few doors down, and I wish I had managed to aim a bit closer to her feet.

"I hope that's just nerves and not morning sickness," she hissed. I wanted to throw up again. "What? You didn't think she was the only one who could overhear things?"

She slammed the door, and Raiden picked me back up. He carried me into his room without another word, and lovingly laid me into his bed before placing the covers over my shaking form.

"Don't leave," I begged him. I thought he would run if he had the chance.

"I'll be right back."

Reaching out with one hand I grabbed his arm. I didn't want to let him go. He slid up next to me on the side of the bed.

"I'm not at all convinced that's the issue,"

he said calmly. "If it is, well, don't worry, I won't be making the same mistake again. Besides, you are innocent in all this."

He pried my hand from his arm and headed back into the hallway.

There is something to be said for those who love you, and are willing to clean the puke, but I didn't hear him clamoring down the hall. I didn't even hear when he slid back into his room later.

I vaguely remember him climbing into his small bed with me. I felt safe in his arms, heart beating near my ear, and I drifted back off to the evenness of his breathing.

Cassandra sat on the end of the bed, her nose turned down to us as I lay against the boy who she lost. For just being a memory, she looked amazingly sad.

"He was willing to forgive you," she sighed. "But not me."

"Compared to your sins, mine are nothing."

Her disdain grew visibly, and I was having a hard time believing there was anything of her left in me. Apart from her love for Raiden and her conflicting feelings for Conrad, could all of those emotions really be mine?

"Isn't there something important you wanted to ask me, Marlow?"

"Several things."

"The baby is dead," said Cassandra.

There was no regret bubbling just below the surface. Not a shadow across her eyes, or a feeling in her voice. Nothing.

"It died before I did," she admitted.

There was still nothing.

"You miscarried."

She was shaking her head before the words had formed in my mouth. She had done something.

"I killed him."

No! my mind shrieked. She had wanted that baby, the baby Raiden wouldn't give her. She had gone behind his back to get what she had wanted and—

"Raiden would never forgive me. I thought he might, honestly. I convinced myself if I could just get rid of it then he would take me back, but the damage was done. I knew even Conrad wouldn't have me when he found out I'd killed it. He loved that thing even more than he loved *me*, if— it's buried in the woods. Tell Conrad by the tree with the moss he loves. He'll know the one."

"You *had* the baby?" I gasped.

How hadn't anyone known?

"I told you, it died before I did. I don't claim to be an expert in our species, I don't know if Hollows are always supposed to be well, Hollow, but when he came out— he was perfect. I was the monster."

She was gone.

When I woke up for good, there were far too many people in his room with us. At least Cassie wasn't one of them. Raiden stood next to me, arms across his chest; pained expression focused on his father who was speaking to someone else I didn't know.

"I'd say it was absolutely impossible."

"Adam, are you sure?" Abraham asked.

"As sure as I can be," Adam shrugged. "The soul transfer went through the same as it always does. The subject is just older, and if you will forgive me I'd rather not continue to talk about the possibility of my dead daughter's baby miraculously implanting itself in some stranger. Especially now that she is awake and staring at me like I've sprouted scales and a second head. Impossible. Look somewhere else for the answer."

Adam was a tall man, maybe a few years younger than Abraham. He carried an antique looking medical bag that he now had clutched tightly to his chest. He was looking at me so intensely, I got the feeling he was searching my soul for any hints at who it once was.

He left the room in a hurry after that. Abraham gave a halfhearted excuse and fled as well.

"See," Raiden said when he and I were all that was left. "Impossible."

I knew before he had said it, but I wished this had been some kind of first time revelation, and I didn't have to hate Cassandra. That I didn't have to hate myself.

Thirty-Two

"I'm not sick," I stated. "I'm not traumatized anymore either. I am allowed out of bed."

I could tell he wasn't budging in his *Marlow must rest* position. I felt a sigh quiver its way into my throat, but I swallowed it down. I didn't want to look like I was doing it in defeat.

"I guess I could stay in bed..." I back tracked. "Do you want to make it worth my while to stay? Say yes, and I'll shut up and do whatever you want."

He laughed. I loved the way it seemed to bounce back from all the walls, echoing across the room and into my chest.

"That sounded awful," I admitted. "I've only known you for five days and I'm begging you to hold me hostage in your bed. What kind of girl am I?"

"Oh," he said with an exaggerated pout. "You're begging now are you? Perhaps I should reconsider my position. Especially as parts of you have known me a lot longer than mere days. Try lifetimes. Several."

I still had no idea how that was possible. In my own mind I was the same person I had been last week, minus the demon boyfriend, and the love of my life. I was starting to understand that it might never make sense. I didn't know if I could live forever that way. How had Cassandra invaded me so completely, but left me so intact?

I loved Raiden without cause. If only the lack of answers didn't make the rest of my life feel so empty. I was perplexed about my attraction to Conrad. Cassie had loved him, mostly because of the life she had carried within her.

What was my excuse?

The more I thought about it, the more I was convinced everything I had done with

Conrad happened because of me, because of a Marlow flaw. Not some soul short circuiting from overuse, but because of me.

It even sounded like me, a complete disaster.

"You're frowning again," Raiden realized. "What are you thinking?"

I didn't know what to tell him. Even if I did, I didn't have the words to do it.

"I'm thinking all the good things I have in my life right now were given to me by Skeleton Lake, but the bad things, that is all me."

"How do you mean?"

"When I look at you," I said running my hand along his jaw for emphasis, and a hopeful seduction. "I forget I'm not perfect. I can feel someone new, better, shining just below the surface. When you aren't around, I'm just the old me. Flawed. I mess things up."

Raiden slid back under the covers with me. He held me so tight, I couldn't move as I waited to see whose bones would break first.

"No one is perfect Marlow, especially me."

I wanted to laugh, if just to release pressure before I split. How could Raiden not be confident in himself? He was kind, forgiving almost to a fault, but there were worse things. In just the little bit I had tasted, he was also a fantastic lover.

"I messed up," he whispered in my ear.

"How so?"

He had done nothing but love me, and ask to be enough as I continued to wrong him. He had loved Cassie too.

"I hated her."

He hated Cassandra. I would have too, but I know he hadn't always.

Sometimes the black walls of Raiden's room had a habit of closing in on me. Now the whole room seemed to cave in.

Cassie had hinted as much, but, how could you really hate the other half of your soul?

"How—" I started.

"It was easy because I hated myself too," he said.

I asked him to tell me the whole story, to start at the beginning. He loosened his arms around me, but he did not let go. We shared a pillow as he told me how he had died.

Raiden had only been two when he had come to Skeleton Lake, and he didn't remember what it had been like to live with his biological family in Idaho. He had parents, and brothers he hadn't seen since being rescued from a hospital death bed near Boise. Raiden had leukemia, and considered himself lucky to not remember being in pain.

When he had been much younger, he had assumed he would end up with Lena, but he didn't explain why he thought that. He just said when it became apparent that she was meant for Alex, he had run away from home. He spent three terrifying hours in the woods alone before anyone had noticed he was missing.

At first, when he realized Cassie was—for lack of a better word—his soul mate, he had been relieved. That was less than four years ago and the relief had been short lived.

Things had gone wrong almost immediately.

"Cassie said she and Conrad used to be best friends."

I could feel Raiden nod against my shoulder, but he wasn't looking at me.

"He would always give her anything she wanted," he whispered. "Anything. He thought their friendship was so unbalanced that he should. She used him, and he let her."

I remembered Conrad had told me that before.

"Do you ever just wish you had given in?" I asked him honestly.

"No. Marlow, we we're so young. I'm still young, and Marlow— you are so much better for me. It makes me feel so guilty that I think that way, like I am making light of death and I'm not. I didn't take her life, she did, but I had already removed myself from it. I was going to let her be happy with him, she just couldn't let herself."

She couldn't have it both ways. She couldn't love and covet him while having his brother's baby. At some point though, she had thought that she could.

Thirty-Three

I didn't want to tell Raiden about Cassie's baby, but I couldn't sneak off to find Conrad without suffering the consequences. Even if I didn't get caught, there would be guilt. Even if I didn't have to lie with breath after breath, withholding information would feel like drowning.

My eyelids hung like weights as I considered my options. I wonder if, as a skeleton, my sleep patterns were doomed to resemble a cat, or other nocturnal creatures. I seemed to keep finding myself awake all night, and then fall asleep whenever I held still too long.

"Raiden?"

"Hmph," he mumbled.

He was asleep, or almost.

"Raiden?"

"Yeah? I'm awake," he said. It was in his usual intoxicating tone, but it wasn't at all believable.

"We should get up."

I tried to encourage him by nudging him toward the end of the bed. It was just like a breeze trying to move a mountain against its will. He wiggled enough for me to squeeze out of his arms. At first I felt the relief of being free, but then I was just cold.

Raiden fell back asleep. He looked exhausted. Purple circles lay under his eyes like fresh bruises, so I left him alone and crept into the hallway.

The smell of vomit had been replaced by the scent of pine. All the other doors upstairs were closed. The house was quiet, but not too quiet. I could tell someone was alive and moving around on the first floor.

I lightly stepped down each step, expecting the wood to scream at me like it did at home. It didn't. The knotted pine was likely just as old, but it seemed less tortured than the boards from my house.

Conrad was asleep on the couch, wrapped in a thread bare blue blanket that was probably the same age he was. He was devoid of his usual smirk, and its absence made him look fragile. I resisted the urge to reach out and stroke his forehead. I had made a deal with myself though, and I could not afford to go back on it.

Someone was banging around in the kitchen, the only hint at life from earlier. I made myself keep walking. It was Abraham, and I was glad. Part of me had known it might be Melissa, but I didn't think I was ready to deal with her. I already might never be able to look at turkey tacos again.

"Need a hand?"

Abraham had raised both Raiden and Conrad. Today he seemed too weak, so broken. It was fast becoming a family resemblance. He would have looked totally unimposing anyway, if I hadn't had a vague idea of what his bones would look like just below his skin.

"Sure," Abraham said, as he slammed another pan down on the stove.

It was then I noticed the tension in his shoulders. The way he had his head held up, like it was the only thing keeping the rest of him erect.

"You um, okay, sir?"

"I'm fine," he tried to assure me.

I didn't believe him.

Abraham tossed me a whisk, and set me mixing pancake batter out of a box, the kind that only required adding water, and the reading capacity of a first grader.

"The boys like pancakes," he said, pulling bacon out of the fridge.

By boys, I assumed he meant Raiden and Conrad.

"Abraham?"

He looked back at me, and I wished I had better prepared myself to ask this question. It sounded ridiculous before I even managed to work it out in my mouth.

"Raiden and Conrad— they used to be friends right?"

I heard him sigh into the giant frying pan he held. He was staring into it like it might solve all his problems, or maybe be the cause of them.

"Of course. They are brothers, and whatever is happening to them now," he said, eying me. "I am confident they will get through, eventually."

Eventually seemed forever away.

I could tell I had ventured onto ground Abraham did not want to cross, and I knew it was only going to get worse.

"I'm afraid I have something to say, and I already know you aren't going to like it."

Abraham turned back from the stove right away. His brown eyes were back to all business.

"Did anyone tell you, that Cassie—her memory, or whatever is left of her—contacts me? Mostly in my dreams?"

He raised his eyebrows at the word *mostly*, but just nodded at everything else. He did not go back to the bacon though.

"She told me something I know Conrad needs to know. Something disturbing. I just don't think I have it in me to break his heart that way."

Again. I didn't say.

He asked me what I was talking about, almost like it was against his better judgment. Given what he knew about his son's deadly love triangle, he was probably right.

As the bacon cracked and sizzled behind him, I brought myself to tears telling him of Cassandra's horrid confession, letting it gush out of my lips like it were my own. Feeling like I had kept it inside too long. Years instead of minutes it had weighed down my hand-me-down soul.

The color had drained out of his face so completely, I expected to the see the skeleton within him without the aid of the lake.

"I'm not sure..." he started, thinking carefully about what he would say.

He was conflicted. I could see it in the lines of his eyes, and the white of his knuckles.

"I'm not sure," he said starting over, more confident this time, "that we should tell him at all."

Abraham seemed like a man who would prefer silence if given the choice, the path of least resistance if at all possible. Did that mean he would seek peace by covering up the truth?

"Why would you say that?" asked a voice from the next room. "Afraid I might do something stupid again? Trying to save me from myself?"

Thirty-Four

As a matter of fact, I was completely consumed by an abiding terror that he would do something rash again, and again it would be my fault. Abraham was fatherly, flowery in his attempt to comfort his son. Which I was sure was *man speak* for something like, "Yes son, I really would have not shared this with you, because I was afraid you would fly off the handle again."

Exactly like he was doing right now.

I took a deep breath that turned into three, before turning to peer into Conrad's eyes.

"I would have told you. I swear."

"I believe you," he said, just above a whisper.

The bacon was now burning; sticking to the pan like it might never come up. None of us moved. Smoke began to fill the kitchen, setting off alarms. Raiden ran down the stairs the second Abraham seemed to snap out of it. In a quick movement he flung the pan into the dishwater, sending steam and grease everywhere.

"What's wrong?" Raiden asked.

Confusion wove its way through his eyes and lips, spilling out onto his tongue.

Conrad opened his mouth to explain, or maybe to say something snide. No words came. He was physically worn down to near collapse, and had been stretched to emotional extremes for likely the last few years of his life. I wished I knew nothing about that, but I did.

"Conrad, you should lay down. I'll tell Raiden."

At the sound of his name his eyes flew back to mine. They had a million accusations as he searched for an explanation, and guilt. I couldn't blame him for jumping to conclusions. That was all me.

Melissa chose that moment to come thudding down the stairs in her purple bathrobe.

"Who is burning down the house this time?"

She said this time, like there had in fact been a slew of other times in which the house had been burned down. Even with knowing Conrad and Raiden so briefly, I couldn't doubt it.

Melissa glanced at Abraham though, like she should have known better. Then she threw her hands up in the air in defeat, and shoved them into the sink to scrub the pan.

Raiden and I snuck out while no one else was watching. Again it was dawn. The sun cracked, sending warm rays of light like a greeting to the cold world. Golden beams danced off the top of the lake before scattering into all the rainbow colors and disbursing back into the air.

We didn't walk to the dock. We didn't leave the yard at all. We stood in the grass that was still dark, and damp with dew below our feet.

"So?" Raiden sighed. He was cold and distant as the middle of a far off forest. He still had the wrong idea entirely, and I could already feel him pulling away.

"It isn't about us."

"Oh, isn't it?" It was a sobering moment, to hear him speak as if he had already made up his mind. To know exactly how thin the ice was I liked to tread upon.

"It isn't," I assured him. "When we were sleeping earlier, Cassie popped into my head again. She— oh God, Raiden, she said that before she died she killed her baby."

He was shaking his head so forcefully I could hear the bones of his neck popping under the pressure.

"She wouldn't. She— Why— it doesn't make sense, I mean she wanted—"

"I know. I did too. As it turns out, she was just a stupid kid who thought she could have it all, and when she realized you would not be letting her back into your life... I think she panicked. She didn't elaborate. She just told me to tell Conrad where she buried the body."

I saw Raiden flinch at the word *body*. I knew he would blame himself for this, just like he blamed himself for Cassandra's and mine unfaithfulness. She was dead, though, and we were all that was left to suffer.

Conrad suffered, because of the child he hadn't known had been born. Raiden suffered, because he took in everyone else's blame, and made it his own.

"Where?" he breathed.

"She said it was under a tree that he liked, one that was covered in moss?"

Raiden's chest was shaking. I could tell he was trying to keep it together.

"She buried her dead baby in a swamp?"

I just shrugged my shoulders. I hadn't known it was a swamp, but if I had been trying to hide something, somewhere no one would look, it would be an ideal place.

"Is Conrad alright?" Raiden asked me seriously.

It shocked me. I hoped that one day, they would be friends again. The sooner the better, but I hadn't thought that such a turn-around was possible.

"I don't know," I admitted. "I can't imagine this being easy. He looked so broken."

"He always looks like that."

When we made it back to the house Melissa had reclaimed the kitchen. Hot pancakes sizzled on the griddle, and thanks to the open windows, the smoke had all but vanished.

Melissa smiled at her son as we walked through the door, and for once I saw the woman below the circumstance. She wore her hatred and bitterness like a cloak to keep certain things out. I couldn't blame her. Maybe the cloak was helping her keep things in, things she wanted to say but couldn't. I didn't know if that was helpful or not.

When her eyes met mine, they were no longer filled with the same loathing as before. I hoped there was still time to change her mind about me.

Thirty-Five

Conrad walked out into the muddy water of the lake. He did not use the dock. I watched him shed layers like every part of him was screaming in pain. His back was turned to me, and I was grateful I couldn't see the parts of him that made him what he was. A Hollow. His skin looked bad enough anyway, with bruises and lacerations dancing, tangled together across his shoulder blades and disappearing below the thick fabric of his shorts.

It had been so little time, but I no longer looked at Conrad with the same eyes as before. When I looked at him now, it was like seeing a broken bit of who I used to be. He was hurt, and that was ripping out the piece of my soul that belonged to him, but I wasn't causing it this time.

Conrad walked into the water slowly, until he stood in the lake, small waves breaking waist deep. Then he was gone. Back into the depths which would hopefully heal his pain.

I prayed that it was working, and no sooner had the thought crossed my mind then I jumped back to the first night I woke up in Raiden's bedroom. He had called the lake a false idol then. What did that really mean?

When Conrad didn't come up right away, I wasn't worried. I just watched from the deck of the blue house anyway.

"He's going to want to go when he gets back," Raiden said from the doorway.

"Abraham said we couldn't go." The other Hollows were still out there.

He snorted before joining me on the edge of the deck. Raiden stopped just behind me. We didn't touch. I could feel the heat radiating off his chest.

"That won't stop Conrad. You know that just as much as I do."

I nodded. I had to admit, I wouldn't have thought a freight train would have stopped Conrad, if I hadn't seen what he had looked like last night.

"I'm going with him," Raiden told me. "He shouldn't be alone."

I agreed. "I'll come too."

He swallowed and chewed loudly on his tongue, as he gazed down at me. Judging my intent, judging how serious I was.

"Marlow," he finally spoke. "I don't think you should go. You've never seen the swamp. It's putrid and dangerous. Trust me when I say you won't like it."

"I believe you, but you are going, so I am too."

Thankfully, he didn't try and argue. He just grabbed me and pulled me into him. Finally, his warmth filled me. I hadn't even wondered what I had really gotten myself into before there was something else to worry about.

"I am so mad at you," Lena called up to me.

The deck, like the rest of the blue lake house, was up on stilts like it was really meant for the beach. Even from the distance I could tell she was furious, and I didn't understand why.

"I told you she was fine." Alex said as he strolled up to her.

"You totally abandoned me for your boyfriend!" she accused me.

Oh right. I had.

"Sorry! I'll be down in a sec."

I sprinted back to the door pulling Raiden along with me. I did not let go of his shirt sleeve until I was sure he was coming on his own accord. I had crafted a plan to get us to the swamp, and I knew Lena wasn't going to like it. She was going to hate it.

I ran through the house, but there wasn't anyone in it to raise an eyebrow in our direction. I raced down the steps and into the yard, colliding with the blond.

"Ouch," she said. She rubbed her arms just for show.

"Come on!" I said pulling her down the shore by her other elbow. She was curious now that there was obvious gossip involved. Really, she had no idea. Alex and Raiden fell into step behind us and remained silent.

We had to get far enough away that no one in any of the houses could overhear us, and so Conrad couldn't sneak up on us through the lake water.

After what I had been through last night, I was going to become a crusader for the end of eavesdropping.

Eventually we found our way to a half circle clearing on the end of the woods. Raiden frowned, and said nothing. He knew true privacy was at a premium. He also knew that it was likely the Hollows were lurking somewhere in these woods that we stood next to.

"So? How was it?" Lena asked, folding her legs beneath her as she sat on a massive tree root.

"How was what?" I asked confused.

"Sex," she said bluntly.

I just stared at her annoyed. Raiden made a noise in his throat. It sounded like a laugh the ended up being closer to choking.

"Lovely," Alex reasoned. "I don't think she brought us out here to tell us about her nonexistent sex life."

I couldn't decide if I wanted to thank Alex, or kill him, so I watched as Raiden lobbed a pine cone at the other boy's face.

It would have been nice to pretend we were normal friends, gearing up for a typical day at the park. No colored bones beneath our flesh. No monsters in the woods behind us.

"Lena," I whispered. "This is important."

Quickly, I replayed last night's events. Leaving out the things that happened before I left Alex's house, and Conrad's disproved theory about the baby.

Raiden didn't bring it up either.

"We should go too," Lena said when I was done.

"We can't," Alex interjected. "Raiden, Conrad, and I, can't all be gone. We can't leave the lake so unprotected. It will be bad enough with them gone."

His voice hinted at disapproval of the plan. He said nothing further about it.

"So, we're the distraction then?"

"If you don't mind," I said, hopeful.

"Oh, I mind. I just don't have any better ideas."

THIRTY-SIX

We left at noon. When it came time to sneak away, Conrad wandered off first. Under normal circumstances, that would have not been unusual, but Abraham did not want him out of the house. So his son had to do the best to persuade him that he was only going out for another swim. With the way he had looked last night, Abraham knew he needed it.

After he was gone long enough that we wouldn't be suspicious looking, Alex, Lena, Raiden, and I set off as well. We said goodbye to the other couple as Conrad swam to meet us on the other side of the lake. His bones showed through his ruined t-shirt and jeans. I didn't even notice.

We were about to do what I know Raiden was dreading.

The sun was almost exactly overhead, and at first it was more than enough to light our way through the trees. When the trees grew taller and closer together, it was like stepping into the night. The temperature plunged with each of our determined steps. Not even snow could have fought its way through the branches above. They were tangled brown masses that let in no light. Their gruesome monster claws kept us in their grasp.

I walked in between the boys, arms across my chest, trying to keep in whatever heat I could retain. I fell several times, but never managed to hit the ground. Raiden and Conrad seemed to switch off, catching me by one arm or the other.

I tried to tell myself that they had been there many times before. Cassie had even managed to get there by herself, pregnant, or recently after giving birth. The thought wasn't as comforting as I was hoping.

Something in the woods did not sit right

with me. It was like walking with a knife in hand, waiting for the carnage. I could tell my companions felt something too, and that they were shrugging it off for my benefit. They were twitchier than normal. I couldn't tell if they were waiting for the fight, or just looking for one.

My hands and feet were numb, just as the echoes began through the woods. It was the wind, I tried to tell myself. It wasn't really, and the sounds around us began closing in.

"Pretty bones that got away!"

"Pretty bones come back to me!"

"Pretty bones are not the worst things in the woods!" they sang.

I knew those voices.

"Ignore the creepers," Raiden instructed.

I really wished I could. Apart from my friends, they were the first monsters I had seen. They were still terrifying to me, and they were laughing at us.

"Enjoy your reign while it still lasts!" one beast clucked with its terrible mouth.

I couldn't decide if it was better or worse that I knew they were here but couldn't see them. I wondered if my imagination captured them as they were in real life.

Conrad and Raiden shared a nervous glance. By the time I looked into their eyes to see what was there, it was gone. We knew the Hollows were likely still in the woods. I'm sure the creepers would like nothing more than for them to scare us all away for good. From what I understood, this was only to be a snatch and grab. Take the girls, and run back to whatever hell they came from. They had nearly killed Conrad last night.

Eventually their voices faded into the dark silence behind us.

I wanted to take Raiden's hand in mine as the pit in my stomach began to grow. I couldn't slight Conrad in such close quarters, especially when there was nowhere to run. I needed that feeling to end before we did, but I didn't want to be the cause of any new wounds.

We could smell the swamp long before any of us laid eyes on it. The fumes wafting from the west smelled like a compost pile, like dead things.

The air here was different. It was hot,

humid, gross, and sticky. I knew the stink of it was likely never to come out of my clothes, and hair, and skin.

All through the forest, I hadn't seen a single living creature. It was still winter, after all, but I hadn't thought about the absence of life until we arrived here.

The swamp was teaming with life, and none of it seemed exactly ordinary.

There were ghost-white, albino rodents that watched us with glowing red eyes as we wandered into muddy pitfalls. I couldn't look away. They were not afraid of us at all, they almost seemed amused.

We avoided the darker water, where the crocodiles parked on the muddy shores. They, too, were colorless as they lay out in the nonexistent sun.

"We're being overly careful," Raiden said. "They can't hurt us."

"That's comforting, I guess. But why can't they hurt us?"

I assumed Raiden was telling me the likelihood of such an attack made it almost impossible. Weren't you far more likely to get struck by lightning than bit by a shark? But your numbers would change if you dangled a bloody arm in front of a great white.

"They just can't," Raiden said before sighing.

"Because they are already dead," he added

I had no idea what to think of that.

The trees here were different too. I forced my mind away from the beasts near me by looking at them. They were almost tropical with their lush green foliage. They should have never been anywhere near Iowa.

"The swamp is fed by underground hot springs," Conrad explained to me quietly.

He didn't have to mention that those hot springs weren't normal. I could feel it in my bones.

The boys obviously knew the way well and yet treaded carefully. I didn't know if it was for my benefit, or because the whole place still felt strange. I didn't really want to know the answer, so I didn't ask. I just kept walking.

Mud was caked to my knees and small brown spots covered most of my exposed skin. I needed a bath, but at least I was no longer cold. My eyes focused on a stream the boys seemed intent to get across. It was small and a sickly, sludgy looking green. We easily got across it in two steps each. I had been so caught up with the water I hadn't even noticed what now stood directly in front of me.

THIRTY-SEVEN

I immediately knew why Conrad liked this tree. It was hollow, with a big gaping hole in its trunk, just like he had. It was covered in a fuzzy layer of green moss, like a second skin, with long tendrils of the green stuff dripping down from its branches like limp skeleton limbs.

"We used to hide things in the trunk," Conrad said as he thrust his hand into the dark hole.

If it had been me, I would have looked first. It didn't seem to be harboring any life that wasn't a fungus.

I watched as Conrad grew still. He was frowning, and then abruptly his whole face fell. At first I thought that maybe there was nothing there. When I looked again I saw him pull something completely encased in his fist out of the trunk.

I don't know what I had been expecting. Cassandra said she had buried the baby. Absurdly, I half thought I would have seen bones too small to be human, too small to have died, held tight in its father's fist.

Conrad looked like a ghost. Haunting the space in front of the hollow tree, silent and unmoving, he was a color sicker looking than white. Clasped in his hand were not bones, but a bit of soggy paper, and some-thing small— metallic.

I heard Raiden gasp from behind me. I didn't turn around, I was afraid that Conrad might just fall to pieces at my feet.

"I was wondering where that had gone," Raiden said flatly.

I had no idea what that was until I saw Conrad dangle it lifelessly from his hand. It glistened red and he rocked it in his fingers until it swung like a pendulum. It was a heart, strung from a simple silver chain. A garnet or a bloody ruby seemed to be entrapped in a tangle of messy wire swirls. Like the heart was caught up in skeleton ribs and fingers just peeking out from behind bones.

Conrad was no longer looking at the heart on a string. His eyes were instead focused on an empty patch of dirt at his feet. It rose as high as the protruding roots next to it, and not even the moss had bothered to grow over it. It was a shallow, unmarked grave.

This time I had to look away. The sound of Conrad falling to his knees on the soft ground soon followed.

All around us the woods were still, like the creatures in it were mourning too. Somehow though, I knew that wasn't right. The air hung so heavily, so thick, I felt the need to cough and gag, to expel it from my lungs before it settled there, churning and burning me from the inside out.

I covered my mouth, intending to do just that when Conrad screamed.

"Run!"

He had sprung from his place before his son's grave. He was dragging me along before

I knew anything was happening. Someone else was in the woods, and they knew we were here too. Raiden paced himself at our heels. I knew he could easily out run me, I could tell he didn't want me to be last. He and Conrad both hastily kept looking behind us.

We ran back through the wetlands of the swamp, mud and water flying like rogue raindrops from our hurried feet. The swamp rats that had so lazily watched us before, unafraid, were now nowhere to be seen. We were running so fast, I didn't even think about the larger predators that could be lurking in our path. I didn't want to.

I was amazing and practiced at running away, but I was terrible at judging distance. I had no idea how far we had come, or how far we had already sprinted back. We were in the heart of the forest now, where I had been so cold before.

I tried to recall how far we had walked before that. I had been treading slowly with a heavy heart, and now that feeling was compounded by the aching in our ribs and the likelihood of our impending doom.

This time, when I hit a tree branch, we

were moving too fast for either of them to catch me. I hit the ground hard.

My pants were torn open by the offending wood, and so was my leg. Blood slid everywhere. The flesh of my shin was mangled and peeled back, like *papier-mâché* from a steel frame. When I saw my bones this time, they weren't glowing, but they weren't broken either. I was in shock.

Raiden scooped me up, just how he had in the stairway, Conrad falling behind him without a word. I slowed us all down. Raiden whispered soft things in my ear that for the longest time I could not make sense of.

"It looks bad," he agreed. "But your bones are fine, see? You're fine. You can run. Marlow, you have to run."

I had to run. I could run, even with a wound like this, as a skeleton. What was keeping me from doing so was all in my head. Just like the need to breathe in the lake— even though I didn't have to. I wiggled my legs out of his arms. Both of my feet landed on the forest floor with a sickening crunch.

Thirty-Eight

Running with your skin ripped open is a weird feeling. Like getting used to the way the wind whistles through a new haircut.

My leg felt lighter as I sprinted, so I wondered how much of my flesh had been left on that tree root.

The sun shone bright ahead of us, teasing me through the breaks of the thinning branches. I wanted to laugh, and scream that we had made it to the canopy overhead. I could almost see the lake just out of the woods.

There was someone else laughing, and I knew it was none of us. A cold, cruel laugh that reminded me of how Conrad had been when I had met him barked in front of us. I recognized the sound of this monster even before I saw his disgusting half face.

"Hello beautiful," he called. "I must say, I rather preferred when you were traveling with that hot blond number. I'm afraid I don't have much use for the male bits of your convoluted love triangle."

"Is talking all you ever do?" Conrad asked, exasperated.

I was starting to suspect the same thing, but I could no longer focus that far away. I tried desperately to clear my foggy vision, but it only made me feel sick. I felt like I was wearing someone else's glasses.

We had been herded like ignorant cows headed to slaughter. Someone had been trailing us, never really intending to catch up, not until we had nowhere else to go. We were injured and exhausted, but I should have known they wouldn't have wanted a fair fight.

"You know," Lance said, "I could have sworn I left you for dead last night. I really hate doing things again and again, so I think this time I'll let Steve here have a go at your ribs while I take care of your leader."

Lance motioned at the boy with Skeleton arms that had come up behind us, and I hated how I couldn't hear him walk.

"I'm a Hollow, the same as you," Conrad said with a shrug. "I have no leader, but I'm sure my brother won't mind kicking your ass if you are too afraid to fight me again."

Lance sneered. The skin of his face stretched grotesquely. Then there was a lot of movement at once. Steve grabbed Conrad from behind, and Raiden launched himself at Lance—who seemed startled that he had made the first move.

I just stood there, unsure of what I should be doing until Raiden yelled at me to run just as the sound of ripping tissue carried through the air to where I was planted. I didn't look back to see if it was us or them. I had the burning sun in my sights and my feet pounding beneath me. I tried to scream for help, but my throat felt like a constricting stretch of desert.

On my third attempt at a yell, something else sprung from my lips instead. It was the same eerie song from the night I had been caught by The Creepers.

My vocal cords vibrated like a wind chime of bones in a breeze as my hand flew up to feel my throat. It would have been soothing if something else hadn't caught my attention.

Alex was running past me. He didn't even look my direction as he flew the way that I had come. Lena stood at the edge of the woods, and I could tell—-even though she seemed to be little more than a white blob at the end of my vision—-that she was frantic.

When I did finally reach her, numb and out of breath, she darted ahead, back toward the direction of the houses. Whether she was running for help, or for her life, I couldn't tell.

My song had cut off and Lena started screaming bloody murder. Oddly, that was comforting; at least she was doing what I could not. People were spilling out of Abraham's house. Many of them were running toward us, and someone-—I assumed Laurel—had begun screaming as well.

Everyone was doing something, and that was when I collapsed. This time, when I hit the ground the darkness was a welcome escape. I knew it wouldn't last.

I had no idea how long I laid in the lawn before anyone realized I was there. I was not the top priority and I didn't want to be. I wanted Abraham to find Raiden and Conrad, and then I wanted them to do whatever you had to do to kill a skeleton.

I didn't want Steve or Lance or anyone of the other Hollows to get away—only because I didn't want to have nightmares about them coming back. I knew I would regardless.

"I drowned," a voice said from the back of my mind. "There are lots of ways to kill a skeleton. All the usual ways, really."

It was Cassie.

"You drowned? I thought you didn't have to breathe when in Skeleton Lake?"

"Not here," she said. "In a ditch."

I was wet, but I didn't know why. Small gentle hands—a woman's hands—held me as I floated on top of the waves. I was very warm, and then I was awake.

THIRTY-NINE

"Melissa?" My voice worked this time, but I rasped because it still felt raw. "Where's Raiden?"

To my surprise, she smiled and, for once, I might have managed to say the right thing.

"With Abraham...and Conrad. He would only go inside if I agreed to take care of you."

"Thanks."

She let me go and I floated, weightless, once more. I tried to think of nothing, but then I remembered I had ripped open my leg on the way here.

Pulling myself up on the dock, I winced. The thought of seeing my skin transparent and torn open seemed even grosser to me than seeing it bloody.

It was fine. There was no longer anything there. I wondered if when my color returned I'd have a scar or a bruise. Right now it was completely intact, even as my bronze leg bone glowed in the middle of it.

"You should stay in longer than that," Melissa said, wading over to me. "You just woke up."

"I want to see the guys. Is Raiden okay? He was about to fight Lance and—"

"Lance is dead."

Melissa smiled like Raiden had shot a prize buck, not killed someone. I knew it had to be done, and I knew that someone had wanted to kill him; I just couldn't minimize anyone's death but my own.

I hadn't grown up in this world, and I just couldn't think of Lance—horrid as he seemed—as something that needed eradicating just because he existed, because I couldn't think of Conrad like that either. Lance was a monster, but his death was still hard for me.

Melissa was just glad he was gone. She

pulled herself on the dock next to me. Her bones that had been exposed glowed a less severe red than Alex's haunting hue—hers were more like sultry lipstick.

"They would have taken you. You would have been made to birth more little beasts or be killed."

I shuddered and held tight to my knees, like I physically had to hold my bones together.

"I know."

I did know.

Melissa walked into her house, still dripping. Since she didn't seem to care, I followed her. She was the only one who lived here likely to yell at me about it, and we seemed to have come to some unspoken truce. I just wasn't sure what it was.

Everyone that lived at Skeleton Lake was in the living room of the blue house. They stood shoulder to shoulder, and sat piled on every available surface. No one was talking. No one was looking at anyone else.

Conrad, Alex, and Raiden were all squashed on the same worn love seat. Lena had perched herself on the armrest next to

Alex, like she was ready to pounce if anyone got too close, but he looked fine. His clothes weren't even ruffled, and I saw no sign that he had been in a fight at all.

My eyes slid next to Raiden's face, and my heart sank. He didn't look up. Something about the way his blue eyes sat down cast staring at the rug seemed so wrong.

His black t-shirt was mostly torn away but there were only small scratches and cuts on his chest and neck. There was also too much blood—but I didn't think it was his.

I made my eyes keep moving, and eventually they settled on Conrad. He seemed fine, apart from the bruising that peeked out above to collar of his dirty shirt. He didn't look back at me. His gaze was fixed on something that was up against the far wall. That was when I noticed the skeleton in the corner.

It was the girl who had talked her way out of harm at my house—the Hollow, Sara. She stood there shaking. I was surprised at first, that I had not noticed the sound of her bones rattling. It sounded like knuckles flying into each other over and over. My heart had been beating so loud that I couldn't hear anything over the sound of my own pulse.

Sara was nervous. Her porcelain skin and dirty blond hair looked sick against the white wall. Evidence of her trek in the woods clung all over her.

"Abraham?" Melissa asked, her usual malice returning to her words, "Why is there a Hollow in my living room?"

My head jerked back, and I could tell by the others expressions I wasn't the only one shocked by her words. There was always a Hollow in her house; she was just choosing to overlook him.

Raiden still hadn't moved his eyes from the floor, but Conrad looked completely put out. No one bothered to answer Melissa and eventually she huffed away upstairs, a door slammed shut behind her.

Still, no one moved. I wondered if anyone else was even breathing.

Lena chose then to look up at me. Her eyes were careful as they caught mine, then she looked back at Raiden. She pulled Alex up by his hand. They had been laced together on the love seat. Neither of them broke the deafening silence of the room, neither of them needed to.

With the seat next to Raiden vacated, I slid in next to him as Alex and Lena escaped out the front door. No one stopped them, and no one even looked at me.

I placed my hand on Raiden's leg that was now pressed up against mine. As he finally looked up, it took everything I had to keep from crying his name.

In his eyes were all my reservations and guilt. I could see it painfully sitting in the stressed whites of his eyes. The death of his advisor had affected him. He didn't seem to be as flippant about death as his mother.

When he looked at me I saw it. Even with the world around us a mess and everyone packed in this room too close.

I realized something in Raiden and I was the same.

Forty

I liked the way Raiden's fingers felt between mine. They were soft, yet still very masculine. Most of all, when they were linked together he felt like an extension of me. I could feel his pulse, and a bit of the tension he felt.

We were both relieved when Abraham asked us to leave the room. We had gotten up together, slowly, but we had already made it to the front door before I heard Conrad object to being thrown out.

Raiden stopped, hand still locked in mine. For a moment I thought he had changed his mind. I could feel the shadows of his thoughts and see them in his eyes.

He seemed to think that maybe he should stay, but couldn't talk himself into it. I didn't want him to.

We walked out into the clean clear air that surrounded the lake, and I gulped it down. I hadn't realized how hard it had been to breathe in the house, as if the dread in the room had been tangible and managed to fill my lungs.

Not another soul was around. Alex and Lena had snuck off. Conrad must have won his fight to stay, because he hadn't followed after us.

Raiden released my hand, but he stayed so close that it was like we were still connected. He took a few more steps, and then completely fell apart.

It took me a painful moment to realize he was crying—not sobbing in a traditional sense—he was hardly making a sound. He had fallen into an awkward position in front of me. His fingers tore at the wet grass from where he lay; the soft sounds coming from his chest seemed to tear him up from the inside out.

Those little noises were burning me. I

had no idea what to do or how to fix this mess, how to fix him. I just hoped that it was possible.

Since I met Raiden—really met him—and woke up here at the Lake, he had seemed so much stronger than me. He faced down one demon after the next. He let me tear again and again at his already weary heart. He had never seemed broken, not until now.

I fell down beside him, wrapping my arms as tight around his shaking shoulders as I could.

"I know you think we're monsters-—but I had never even thought of killing someone before. Not even a Hollow," he whispered into my shoulder. "Some of us don't think —-they talk about them like they are less than us—like..."

"I know."

I knew exactly what he was thinking. No matter what happened to Conrad and Raiden, no matter how much they had hurt each other, Raiden would always love his brother. He would never think of Conrad as any less of a person than he was.

In the middle of my belly, the part that

had been so knotted up seeing Raiden crumble, I understood something I hadn't before.

I hadn't loved Conrad for myself, or even because of Cassie. I had loved him because—

The door slammed behind us. The bang was so loud it seemed to push Raiden even further into the ground, but I jumped up immediately.

Conrad was standing with his back pressed up against the poor screen door so hard, I could hear the sound of the fabric screaming loudly as it tore from the frame.

He was flushed, like he'd picked yet another fight. He was also staring at nothing like the blankness was his own worst enemy before turning around and kicking the side of the house.

"What's wrong?" I gasped.

I had to know, I also thought the answer might kill me and further wound Raiden, but I had to. I didn't know how I'd handle both of them falling apart.

"That girl saved my life," he said. "The Hollow girl."

"Sara," I said, because she had a name and I was going to use it.

He nodded.

"She saved me that night I went after Lance alone. Then she came back with us without a fight, and now..."

"And now they want to kill her," Raiden said as he pulled himself upright.

I looked back at him, horrified. I knew he wouldn't be joking.

"Conrad, please stay with Marlow outside while I fix this."

"No! I need to come with you!"

"Marlow, please," he pleaded. "Please just do this one thing for me. You know, I know better than to try and make you do something you don't want to."

So I stayed behind when he walked up, and pushed his way through the screen door. The black mesh was now mostly torn from the frame and flapped behind him in the wind.

I had no idea why he didn't want me to go with him and it was unnerving.

"What's he going to do?" I asked Conrad, who now chose to lean up against the house instead.

He looked at me blankly; all of the

longing and lust seemed forgotten. All I could see in them now was darkness.

"He's going to go pull rank on the old man."

"Huh?"

I had no idea what Conrad meant by pulling rank. I imagined me trying to tell my parents what to do, and then I imagined me failing and being grounded for life.

"Dad has to do it," he said, as if that cleared anything up.

"He has to?" I asked dubiously.

I wondered if perhaps Abraham was indebted to his son for some reason, but I still couldn't imagine him just doing as he was told.

"Because he's the leader," Conrad added.

My eyebrows slid together. "Abraham?"

Conrad sighed at me like I was an idiot. "Raiden."

FORTY-ONE

"Raiden is just a kid. We're just kids."

Conrad was laughing, and part of me was glad to see the return of his semi-sadistic smile, along with the color to his face. I was also furious he seemed to be laughing at yet another joke I wasn't in on.

"They told you how we ended up at this happy but Halloween-esque existence right?"

"The souls?" I asked.

He nodded, his smile gone again.

"Alex told me that they belonged to a group of people who knew what the lake really was. Which is great and all considering

I don't even know what it really is. All I know is I have half of some dead girl's soul."

I watched as Conrad stood up further, pulling away from the side of the house. I thought he would step closer to me, be he didn't.

"No one knows what the lake is as a whole, but we know many of its parts. It is an energy creator, and destroyer—it is many things and none of them at the same time."

I swallowed thickly. The word *destroy* seemed to hang in the air.

"Raiden says the lake is a false idol."

"He is absolutely right."

I wondered, was it alive? Could it hear us?

Raiden's words echoed through my thoughts like the wind that blew around us. "What it gives to us, it can so easily take away."

"Will it kill us?" I whispered.

"No," he paused. "It needs you every bit as much as you needed it."

I noticed he said you, and not we, but I didn't bring it up. None of this explained why Raiden was the leader, so I said as much.

"The people who first discovered this lake were a tribe, a group of warriors. They had a chief."

"Okay?"

"And that is whose soul Raiden has—-you too, I guess."

So Raiden was the leader just because the person who had his soul originally had been?

"I'm not explaining this right," Conrad said flopping himself back onto the house. "Ask Raiden about it later... a lot later... and when he's in a better mood."

That was not a problem. Of all the many things I wanted to talk to Raiden about, him being some kind of warrior chief was not high up on my to-do list. The first thing I wanted to ask Raiden was if the Hollows had all gone, and if he was sure either way. Since Conrad was here now, I asked him instead.

"I have no idea," he answered. "I'm afraid there is worse news."

I didn't think I would ever be ready for worse news, but I waited for him to tell me anyway. I started at him until he looked back at me, pleading with my eyes for him to just say it—to just do it without me having to ask. Because I wasn't sure if I could.

"There are other Hollows."

I looked for something in his words that wasn't there. I was thinking he was talking about himself—making a joke about how dangerous and awful he was—-but he wasn't.

"They live somewhere in Nevada, a whole huge group of them, which is just insane. Sara says that Lance was important to them, and that there will likely be some kind of retaliation, and soon.

Oh no. Raiden could barely handle ending one of their lives, if they came here looking for a fight I didn't know what would happen.

My knees felt weak, but so did the rest of me. I meant to sit, but as drained as I was all I could really do was collapse. Conrad was by my side before I felt myself fall. It seemed like I was always falling. He was trying to stand me back up, but I didn't want to. I wanted him to tell me it was a joke, but I knew he wasn't kidding.

When I had first met Conrad, all I had

wanted to do was wipe that stupid grin off his face, but now I wanted its return.

Conrad gave up on getting me on my feet and pulled me close to his hollow chest. His heart beat rhythmically as his breath tickled my neck. He seemed far too solid to be made of so many holes.

"It will be alright," he breathed, sending several of my curls flying into the wind.

It didn't feel like it would though, and I kept thinking I was the one that should be filled with holes as I was so empty feeling.

"What are you doing?" Raiden asked.

He stood on the other side of the battered screen door, suspicious, be there was no need to be. I could hardly muster the energy to object as Conrad told him I had fainted.

"I didn't faint," I mumbled. "I fell."

But Raiden had already shot to my side and pried me from his brother's grasp. I hating making him worry, but I was so tired.

"I was just scared," I admitted.

"Why?" he asked.

His arms tightened around my arms and chest, and I wanted to poke at him for being too over protective but that seemed like too much work.

"You know why," I managed, but I could barely breathe in his embrace. I didn't know if that was because of the physical hold on me, or the emotional one.

"You told her," Raiden said to his brother.

"I asked."

Conrad headed back into the house, and all he said was a whispered, "Thank you," just before the door slammed shut behind him.

Raiden and I walked back to the lake.

Forty-Two

"It helps if you keep telling yourself he's the bad guy."

I jerked so hard that the top of my skull slammed into his chin.

"Ow," he hissed, but he wasn't bleeding, just looking at me like I was insane, so I guessed he was alright.

"How can you say that about your brother?" I demanded.

"I'm sorry?"

"Wait," I mumbled, as I got the feeling we weren't talking about the same thing at all. "What are you talking about?"

He sighed roughly, obviously regretting that he had said anything at all.

"It makes me feel a little better if I keep reminding myself that Lance was the bad guy."

He thought I was distressed over Lance's death, and I was, but that wasn't it entirely. I didn't know if I should tell him I had been thinking of Conrad. Even though it was innocent, it still felt wrong.

"I just keep thinking of what he wanted to do to you. He was so horrible. I don't even think I can hate him properly."

I opened my mouth, maybe to tell him that hating a dead person was hardly worth the effort, but only ended up pressing myself further into his chest and mumbling something incoherent into his neck.

My moments with Raiden tended to be more perfect when the world fell down around our shoulders. The breeze made his scent mingle with mine. It was a habit I needed to escape.

As Raiden began trailing kisses down my shoulder, I knew it didn't matter. I would endure a thousand catastrophes if this was what waited at the end of them.

There was a heat within me that felt like

every drop of blood I had was screaming for him. Something, I supposed, science would never understand

And it was comforting to know that Raiden would endure as many catastrophes for me—if not more, and that we weren't unbalanced. Even though I felt so weak, I would do anything for him and that made me stronger.

Raiden cupped my face in his hands, and pulled me up until I met his eyes. I watched as he scanned over me, like he was checking for fault lines that were threatening to rip me apart, but with him so close I felt more complete than I had my entire life. Such a wild idea that he did have the other half of my soul, yet there could be no doubt. There had never been a feeling like this before I came to Skeleton Lake.

He kissed me roughly, and both our lips were too dry. I thought mine might split under the desperate pressure, but blood wouldn't be enough to make me stop.

The sun was setting behind the trees. A bright ball of molten light seemed to be rising off the edge of the world despite that it was really sinking behind it. Everything was glowing, but I only noticed because it was reflected back at me in Raiden's eyes.

I had no idea how another day had passed, but it did, and I hadn't even watched. At least until we were disturbed.

Abraham stepped out of the screen door behind us with a crash. I blinked, thinking Conrad had returned, but he hadn't. Raiden's father stood like a furious-faced statue, like an avenging angel that was about to ruin the rest of our lives.

"If you want to keep her around so much —" he spat, and I assumed he had been talking about me, "you have to watch her!"

I frowned, I wasn't sure how much closer he could watch me then when his tongue had been down my throat.

Then I looked over his shoulder, and I understood he had meant another *her*.

Sara hung back in the doorway like a poor kicked little dog. Her arms were wrapped around her whole thin frame and dirty hair still spilled into her face.

So that's why he was so angry. Raiden had intervened to keep this girl alive when his father had other plans—one that would have ended her existence.

It was hard not to look at all of them in a different light, even though the sun had finally been extinguished. The night was growing dark, and the shadows more haunting.

In a world where everyone was good or evil, and everything was cut and dry, decisions would be so much easier. In my new world of beautiful bones, and false flesh everything lay in shades of grey. Not really good or evil but bits of both.

Sara had never hurt any of us, and judging by her lost doe eyes, I doubt she ever would.

"Fine," Raiden said.

He did not sound bitter or annoyed as he stood up straighter, but I had to admit that I was. My time with him was always being interrupted.

For once I just wanted to finish a moment with him, and for that I would go through almost anything.

I had already died once. Nothing but the thought of losing Raiden was worse than that.

"Are you hungry?" Raiden asked as we walked back inside.

I was starving. I hadn't eaten since the breakfast Melissa had managed to save, but Raiden wasn't talking to me. When Sara answered it was hardly above a whisper, "I haven't eaten in two days."

Forty-Three

Raiden was as shocked as I was. He was angry, whereas I was only struck silent. I could feel the rage pulsing around him like the thick, dark bands of a hurricane.

Lance had dragged his people around the woods, stalking us, waiting for an opportunity for days and he hadn't even fed them. He was a monster, and this was the first time since I had heard the news that I was glad he was dead.

I waited for the guilt to come sloshing in after my revelation, but it never did. I tried to use that as proof I was right.

The three of us straggled into the living

room just as the reminder of the group decided to take their leave. There were still so many people I knew nothing about, but it just wasn't the right time to ask.

I wondered if it would ever be.

We headed back to Melissa's kitchen, which had been returned to perfection since breakfast. I could still smell cleaner covering the odor of burnt bacon—and I was so hungry, it was almost appealing.

We might share a soul, but Raiden was still infinitely better in the kitchen than I was. He let me help with the ham sandwiches, though. I could tell Sara struggled to keep her manners, but I wouldn't have minded if she had swallowed her food down in one loud gulp, or even if she had managed to take a bite out of Melissa's flower lined china. I was happy to see that some of it managed to survive Laurel's visit.

Just looking at Sara made me hungrier, and my stomach didn't even know that was possible. I couldn't wrap my head around what she had been through.

We sat in the kitchen in silence until Conrad wandered in halfway through the meal. I watched as he glanced at Sara out of the corner of his eye, but he blinked back to Raiden when he saw me looking at him.

"What?" he said to his brother. "No one made me a sandwich?"

He was kidding. I could easily tell from the tone of his voice if I hadn't seen his smile, or the humorous way he placed his hands on his hips in phony exasperation; but Sara jumped up anyway. Intending, it seemed, to make him one.

"He's kidding," Raiden said. "Conrad, tell her you're kidding."

"I'm kidding," he breathed, but his voice had gone so low it was practically unrecognizable.

Sara looked dubious, but she did eventually sit back down. I wondered if she was trying to impress Conrad, or if she was just so used to being barked orders that it was habit.

"As far as I'm concerned, you are now a guest here. Guests don't have to work in our house," Raiden tried to explain.

"You are the strangest group of Skeletons I have ever seen," Sara mumbled.

Something was itching at the back of

mind, something I had wanted to ask but that had slipped through the chaos my head had been swimming in since coming here for the first time. It was like liquid though, and as soon as I thought I had a good grasp it would slip through my fingers.

"And how many have you seen?" Raiden asked calmly—far more composed than I could have ever managed. We had trouble with a small group of them, I didn't know if I wanted to dwell on the numbers.

"I know there are others; and if I didn't you would be proof of that—but I have no idea where, or how many, or even why they exist. Where are you from, Sara?"

"I've lived my whole life on the shore of The Dead Sea."

Somehow, that made too much sense. Everything about Skeleton Lake was alive. The forest that surrounded it was filled with life, and nothing but the swamp even hinted that creatures like us resided near it. The Dead Sea was well, dead. Nothing lived around it.

"I thought you lived in Nevada," Raiden said.

My mind ground to a halt. I had been conjuring postcard-worthy images of The Dead Sea in my head. They were so vivid I swore I could smell the salt, and feel the grit of it against my skin.

When I had stayed outside with Conrad, when Raiden had gone to save Sara's life, Conrad had said that Sara lived with the group of other Hollows in Nevada.

"That's where the real Dead Sea is," Sara said with a laugh.

I didn't know what to think of that. As far as I knew Nevada was made of mountains, and deserts, and neon lights. Of course, until last week I had thought that Skeleton Lake was a cornfield.

"And you've seen other places as well?" Raiden asked her.

She quickly nodded her head yes, sending her dirty locks further into her eyes.

"Only one other with my own eyes, but —it was enough. I've been told of others..." Sara trailed off.

Her eyes seemed to shrink further into her skull. The silence drug on as if it were days, and not just awkward moments in which the Hollow girl seemed to decay before our eyes. Like a real corpse.

"Raiden," Conrad nearly growled, "I don't think she wants to talk about it."

I watched as Raiden opened his mouth to protest, but I knew it was only halfhearted. He never said a word as he shut his mouth and shook his head. The bone creaked in his neck like a door in need of oil, but no one mentioned it as I let my eyes wander back to Sara.

"No," she said. "It's okay I should probably talk about it, since I wasn't even allowed to before."

I frowned, what did she mean she couldn't talk about it?

Sara took a deep breath that sounded more like a ghastly wind whipping through the room than one broken little girl.

"I didn't want to come to Skeleton Lake," she began. No one said a thing.

"I was born on the shore of The Dead Sea, and I never wanted to leave. I didn't want to be different. Lance used to fill my head with so many stories. Stories of faraway places, and people who'd look down on us; I knew there were others because my mother is not a Hollow, she came across the bridge of bones and ice long before I was born."

The temperature in the room plunged as we all imagined what such a bridge might look like. Goosebumps covered my flesh as I shook. I had grown accustomed to seeing bones at Skeleton Lake, but something about the bones of dead things would never agree with me.

"A bridge of bones and ice?" Raiden asked softly.

Sara nodded her head, "I know it sounds strange, but I've seen it, and I hope to never go back."

"Where does it go?" Conrad asked.

Such a logical question, my mind fumbled with the possible answers, it had been too caught up with the grotesque logistics to realize it must surely lead somewhere.

"To the top of the world," she said with ice in her voice. "To the glacier forest."

I could tell Sara had reached the point she dare not continue, and I was pleased that neither of the boys attempted to press her further and quickly changed the subject.

"Tell us about your mother," I said.

Sara only tensed, "I don't want to talk about her," she whispered. "I have to tell you about Christian before I lose my nerve."

"Who's Christian?" Conrad asked, almost too interested.

"Lance's dad."

My heard sank. The person that would likely seek us out for revenge. Conrad was nothing like Abraham, but I worried what Christian must be like if the apple that was Lance had not fallen far from the tree.

"He's worse," Sara half sobbed. "Way worse than Lance. I know that seems impossible after what he tried to do to you—but left alone, without influence from his father, or expectations he could never hope to meet, Lance was a different person. Every bit of hell I have ever been through was because of Christian. He wants everything, but will give up nothing. Only he is perfectly fine sacrificing the rest of us—and that cost him his son."

I glanced back to Raiden. He had gone pale. A suffocating tension hung in the air.

No one knew what to do or what to say—no one knew what we should do now.

Abraham stomped into the kitchen to glare at us, only to stomp right back out again. I couldn't decide if he was still livid with Raiden, or would always behave this way around Sara, but I was coming close to hating him for it.

"I should just tell you," Sara breathed. "You should know." She took another shaky breath. The rest of us didn't even breathe.

"The first story my mother ever told me was about her home in the Glacier Forest. To get there you have to cross the bridge..."

"Of bones and ice," I repeated quietly, and she nodded her head.

"It's an island, but it wasn't always where it is now. Everything on it used to be alive, but now it's all frozen. The trees have shattered off at unnatural angles—they look petrified. Everything there is wrong, including the people; and that's coming from me."

Sara pushed her hair briefly out of her face, exposing her hollow places. I couldn't even imagine that there were creatures more wrong than Hollows.

"Why did you go there?" Raiden asked. His voice cracked horribly, like he wasn't sure he wanted to know the answer. Sara just shrugged.

"The same reason we came here. The same reason we go anywhere, really. Girl Hollows can't have kids. I guess we aren't human enough. That is the thing Christian wants more than anything else. That's the reason he's going to come here."

FORTY-FOUR

January passed into February. It was Valentine's Day, but I was wearing black—a habit I picked up from Raiden and Alex, who almost exclusively wore that color.

As I attempted to glide down my rickety farm house stairs, my father took one look at my long dress and mumbled something about mourning under his breath. My eyes were only for Raiden.

He stood against the front door, wearing pants with too many buckles to count, and a completely see-through shirt—if that's what it was—peeking out from under his black leather jacket. I was surprised my parents hadn't commented on his clothing, but I sure wasn't complaining.

In Raiden's grasp, something he held too tight crinkled; I still didn't look away from his eyes.

"You look even more amazing than you usually do."

I laughed warmly as I felt red pool in my cheeks. These days he saw my bones more than the rest of me, but at least I had grown used to them. It was unfathomable that even in such a short time, I couldn't remember an existence apart from this. Even here, standing in a house I had visited so many times as a child.

Every day with Raiden felt as though it was my first and millionth day with him, and I hoped that feeling never stopped. The spark between us thus far refused to wane, and I had learned to appreciate it—and my life—so much more.

We were going to the Valentine's dance put on by my church in town, and I was sure they would absolutely hate Raiden's attire. I hoped they hated it enough to kick us out. There was nothing I would relish in more than going back to Raiden's house and spending another lazy evening at the lake. The nights had begun to bleed together, but they were all amazing.

Unfortunately, Lena loved to dress up, and if there was one thing I had learned about my new friend, it was that she was unaccustomed to hearing the word "no." So we went. Lucky for her, the look in Raiden's eyes alone was enough to make it worth it.

When my parents finally released us, we wandered into the cold. Snow still littered the ground. A good thaw seemed months and months away. Raiden led me by my cold fingertips to an unfamiliar black car.

"Mom's," he said as he opened the door for me.

I had yet to ask where she had been before the Hollows had come to Skeleton Lake—and I doubted that it was really any of my business. She was here now, and I knew that was in some part because I was here and she thought she needed to watch me. I should hate that, but I understood.

Raiden drove far slower than usual. The flashy black Mercedes might have looked better than the rusted green Jeep, but it didn't handle as well in the snow.

The sky above us was starless, and gray instead of black. The sun had been set for hours, but it seemed as though it wanted to snow again soon. We did not speak on the way, instead opting to sit in comfortable silence as winter farmland turned into a one-horse town. Then my phone rang, shattering the content air around us like it was a fragile glass and reminding us of the other people in our world.

"Lena," I said, though he probably could have guessed.

A few of my old friends had eventually come around after that night at Rachelle's—but I learned all too quickly the difficulty of keeping secrets. Especially ones of this magnitude. It became obvious why Raiden, Alex, and Lena had always kept to themselves. It was far less complicated, and there was never a need for excuses.

"Where are you?" Lena yelled.

I could hear the parental approved music blaring behind her, as if the volume alone could somehow make it cooler.

"Almost there," I sighed.

"Good, there is this girl here..."

"Yeah?" I asked, unsure where she was going with that line of thought.

"She's got my dress on, the one from homecoming."

I hadn't attended that dance, I hadn't cared to, but I did remember a conversation on my couch where she had told me about it. It felt like a lifetime ago. Could it really have only been last month?

"The pink one?" I asked. I really thought that Lena was going to freak out about someone wearing the same dress as she was now. I was surprised to hear she was bothered by this connection.

"I don't mean it's the same style of dress, I mean, it the same exact one. Mom altered the straps and I'm sure it's the one. She must have donated it to goodwill or something."

People in our town were poor, there wasn't but one street light, but there were three thrift stores. I wasn't surprised at all.

"So?" I asked.

"So.... I guess you're right, it doesn't really matter. I just like my stuff."

"Right, well, we're in the parking lot so I will see you in a few."

Raiden had bought me a corsage. He had squished its plastic case while he had waited for me downstairs, but it was still beautiful. Snow crunched below my spiky black heels, my feet hurt horribly already and I had taken exactly three steps.

I hoped to only make an appearance then leave as quickly as possible. Somehow, I knew with Lena it would never be that simple.

After paying for our tickets, the first thing I saw from the corner of my eye was a glowing red light. I nearly gasped, but when I turned to look at it I noticed it was only Lena's red dress shimmering explosively in the strobe lights behind her.

Alex stood lagging behind as she ran toward us. I noticed he was wearing a black t-shirt with a tie that matched Lena's dress—and his completely concealed bones—perfectly.

"You guys dress so weird. Why are we friends again?" I teased.

"Have you seen a mirror? Besides, you're just as weird as us on the inside."

And I supposed that was what really mattered, but Raiden shoved him playfully up against the wall anyway. Two chaperones in the corner briefly stopped talking to scowl at the two boys. This was going to be a long night.

I really didn't feel like dancing, ever, but Lena dragged me to the dance floor anyway. Last time I ruined my feet with shoes I had ended up in Skeleton Lake, and I hoped this night ended the same way. At least this time I knew the Lake would heal them.

The DJ—who appeared to be someone's brother, finally switched to some lyric-less techno after losing the constant battle with parents over what was appropriate content. The beat was throbbing, and complicated, but it may have just been my heart beating against Raiden's.

I liked that I hadn't got used to the feel of him yet, and I hoped that I never would.

The girl wearing Lena's dress passed by us then. She, too, was small and blond, but I doubt she pulled it off as well as my friend had. Lena caught sight of the girl and decided it was as good a time as any for a punch break.

Someone's somber looking father stood guarding the punch bowl like it was a matter of national security, and he had the look of a marine that was slightly passed prime. Somehow he never blinked. It was hard not to laugh. I did my best to avoid looking guilty, but the man looked at us suspiciously anyway, and seemed to label us trouble makers in his head.

By ten, the dance was completely dead and I was overjoyed. If we hurried, I could have my feet fixed and spend close to two hours at Raiden's without my parents even wondering where I was.

I had been close enough to taste it, too.

We had left the dance in a fit of laughter, and lungs weighed down with the cold, cold air as we escaped; but by the time we turned onto the road that would lead us to Skeleton Lake, we knew something was very wrong.

Flashing lights reflected off of the gray sky like the air held close laid walls. Fire trucks, ambulances, police cars, news crews, too many vehicles to count, too close together, too overwhelming.

Alex and Lena were in the car in front of us. I watched as Alex rolled down his window to talk to a police officer, but I couldn't make out what they said. I knew they were arguing about something. Finally, Alex gave up and turned around. It wasn't exactly easy on the narrow two lane road, but he managed and Raiden quickly followed suit. As the black Mercedes whipped around, I caught a glimpse of familiar pink taffeta lying in the ditch.

FORTY-FIVE

My phone was ringing again.

"Did you see...?" Lena whispered.

I only nodded but I knew she understood.

"Ssh!" Alex hissed. "No talking until we get back to Marlow's."

And no talking about it there, either. I wanted to scream. We could go back to my house, and we had to, but there would be absolutely no gossip of dead girls in my house. If my parents found out, they might never let me leave it again. Not that tight lips would save me for long—there were no secrets in this town. Except for maybe mine, and skeletons dumped into the front yard weren't going to help me keep them.

My parents were surprised to see us return so soon, and I hoped my fake smile looked more convincing than it felt. Darkness seemed to stifle the lamp light in the living room as we all sat awkwardly on the couch. Our shoulders were touching, I could feel both Raiden's and Lena's heavy breathing— it seemed like it hurt.

Alex turned on the television, I thought he'd be looking for the movie channels to distract Lena, but he flipped to the late news instead. The scene was familiar. The blinding lights on the screen weren't as captivating as they had been in real life, but I wasn't looking at them. I was staring at the closed ambulance doors, afraid of what horrors could be behind them.

My father said goodnight without looking at the news report. He followed my mother into their bedroom and shut the door behind him. I listened carefully until I heard their lock slide into place.

"That fleshies' bones were showing,"

Alex said to the TV, "but we know she looked fine a couple of hours ago..."

I felt acid eating its way from the stomach to the back of my tongue. This was just like the words that had been burned into the school. It seemed like far too much of a coincidence. "Stop talking about her like she's some kind of meat!" I said. "She's a person and something terrible has happened to her—and it's probably because of us!"

"Shh," Raiden said soothingly. I had been wailing over the sound of the continuing news.

I didn't want my parents to hear, not really. I just couldn't make myself worry they might. I'd have no explanations, not ones that wouldn't make me look guilty. Even if I hadn't been the one who did the horrible deed, my heart still felt that we were responsible. I knew that feeling wouldn't stop, not until I found out what had been done to her and made sure it never happened again.

All and all the information on the news was lacking. We had gotten more information from our ill-fated drive down County Road Nine.

What we knew so far though amounted to very little. Another blond in Lena's dress had been stripped down to her bones in less than two hours.

"When was the last time we saw her?" I said, wanting to sure up our time frame.

"When we saw her on the dance floor, when I said we should get punch," Lena said, "but that doesn't mean she has been missing since then. I didn't even see her leave." That was true, so all we knew was she had either left the dance on her own, or that someone had taken her shortly after that. "Alex, you should call my dad."

"Shouldn't you—" Alex started, but Raiden cut him off.

"He's not really speaking to me at the moment." Raiden meant he hadn't spoken to them since Sara had come to stay at Skeleton Lake, but none of us needed further clarification, so Alex got out his phone and wandered into the kitchen. "I guess I'll call Conrad," Raiden mumbled as he slid into the couch.

The springs groaned beneath us, and I felt like we were all stuck in quicksand, being pulled down together.

"He's with Sara. Maybe this is... maybe she knows..."

He didn't have to say it; we were all thinking the same thing. That payback had arrived.

Alex paced in the other room, the linoleum complaining loudly with his every step. The longer he stayed on the phone with Abraham the more agitated he grew, and the faster he paced.

"We don't even know if this has anything to do with us." Lena said meekly. I could tell by the hunch in her shoulders she couldn't believe that, no matter how badly she needed to. I knew she realized how lucky she was that she hadn't been killed and left in that ditch—but that was at such a high cost.

Raiden sighed. "A skeleton gets dumped less than a mile from your house, and you hold out hope that it's a coincidence? That'd be fantastic if not for the fact that it's not damn likely."

Lena let out a pitiful sob into a throw pillow, and I heard Alex stop pacing long enough to glare in our direction. Raiden called Conrad.

"Something is wrong," he hissed into his phone. "We're at Marlow's. No, you can't come here. We don't know what else is in the woods and the road is—you saw? How close? And I am going to assume you didn't care how dangerous that was. Fine, whatever you say. Call us when the road is clear."

Raiden looked like he wanted to crunch his phone, but had thought better of it. He was still half sunk into the couch, so instead he halfheartedly loped his phone to the coffee table. It seemed to sail through the air in slow motion before sliding across the smooth top and clattering to the floor. Alex stopped pacing again.

"What did he say?" I asked, hoping that it wasn't personal; and that rehashing it wouldn't make him want to crunch something else.

"He said that they didn't know who was behind this—but that they could guess. Conrad said he walked down to the edge of the lake. Not the edge of the water, but the magical edge that separates what is in the real world from the illusion that hides the lake and the area around it. He walked right up to it and watched as they removed that girl—Hanna's remains. They don't know who she is yet, and they are way off. They are assuming she had to be dead for a while because the only thing left is bones. Only that doesn't explain the dress, because it was apparently untouched."

None of us wanted to breathe, but I heard my father snoring in his room sound asleep.

"They went to Lena's, but they don't think there is a connection. They just think that the killer needed someplace desolate to dump her."

I cringed, knowing that this wasn't random, that it couldn't be.

This has been done to tell us something.

Forty-Six

Lena and I lay curled together on my bed, Alex kicked back in the recliner, and Raiden stayed exactly as I left him on the couch—trying to disappear into it. None of us slept well.

It snowed through the night. Wind blew white powder in a slant against the house as frost climbed up the windows. The grisly sounds of winter haunted us, but the house was eerily quiet on the inside, especially as it held so many extra people. It was like we were all still holding our breath, straining our ears for what must surely be lurking in the dark.

Just after four in the morning, Raiden's phone rang. I tensed and held tight to Lena as she held tight to me. We wouldn't help anything but thundering down the stairs at this hour, and if it was something terrible he knew where to find us.

"This is my fault," Lena said below the covers. "I wished something bad would happen to her and it did."

"It's not your fault," I argued. "You couldn't have known, and besides, you didn't mean it."

There below my old quilt, with Lena's sweaty fingers wrapped too tight around my wrists, I finally drifted off to sleep. At first there was only the comforting solitude of darkness, and stillness of being alone in my head. That is something you can't possibly miss until it's taken away from you.

Then, as if just to spite me, she was there.

"You sure do like trouble," Cassie quipped, and I mentally huffed.

Sure, says the girl who killed herself. She tutted loudly, and I assumed that meant that she could hear me without having to talk.

"He needs you. I hope you realize that, Marlow," she said. I did, but I didn't say it, and Cassie only sighed. "Someone is watching you through your bedroom window."

She vanished.

I jerked awake a split second before Lena. The sound of the top of her head slamming into my chin seemed to vibrate off all the walls in my room, only it was probably just vibrating in my skull.

"What are you doing here?" Lena yawned before plopping herself back into my bed.

I supposed that meant this wasn't a life threatening intruder.

Conrad hovered in the swirling February snow, but I knew he was standing by on the giant oak tree like he had before. I climbed out of bed, and flew open the window.

"What are you doing here?" I repeated.

Paying my thin pajamas no mind, I motioned for him to come in out of the cold, but he didn't move. I wondered about his hesitance before following his eyes down to the ground. There in a snow drift stood the thin frame of a girl, and I knew at once it was Sara.

"Raiden keeps hanging up on me," Conrad complained from the tree branch, and I nearly laughed out loud. He had come all this way in bad weather to tell me that?

"Raiden's having a moment," Lena mumbled, her head firmly under my favorite pillow. I scowled at her, even though I knew she couldn't see me. At least it made me feel better.

"He's not having a moment. Okay, we are all having a moment. Besides, I am sure he is only hanging up on you because you did something to piss him off—again," I said.

And for just a moment, Conrad looked almost embarrassed. I supposed there is a first time for everything.

"Anyway," he said, changing the subject. "The road's clear. When are you coming home?"

"Conrad, this is my home. I can't just sneak off in the middle of the night."

He smirked at that, and it was so very Conrad I was consumed by the overwhelming urge to punch him in the face—but at least his lopsided grin no longer tugged at my heart strings like it had before. In the past month, whatever feelings that I still had for Conrad were locked in the vault of a brother I never had, and I knew he felt the same.

"Who are you?" he asked. "And what have you done to the real Marlow?"

I chewed the inside of my cheek to keep from laughing at his corny joke. I didn't want to laugh, with my window opened wide to the dark and scary places below it. Only I knew exactly what he was talking about. I had snuck out this very window more times than I could count on a hand, and one such time he even warned me better.

The new Marlow just valued her life so much more. She also had a good reason not to find herself grounded.

"We'll come as soon as everyone wakes up. I have to stick around long enough to assure my parents I didn't do anything they will live to regret."

He snickered as snow flew around his face and onto my bedroom floor.

"You didn't come through the woods did you?" I said, grabbing his arm before he could turn and climb down.

"Nah, took the Jeep. Left it parked up the road."

I just nodded, but I hated thinking he would brave the woods after Raiden had expressed concerns over what could be hidden in them.

"Conrad? Is this... I mean could it be...?"

"Sara doesn't know for sure if it's him, but if she had to guess..."

"Right," I breathed. "Alright, thanks," I said as he quickly descended the tree. I shut the window soundlessly behind him, but Lena was already sitting up on my bed.

"I hope you don't expect me to go back to sleep now," she said between yawns. "Let's go watch TV."

Before I could focus enough to remind her that the boys were trying to sleep down there, she had climbed from the covers and had begun treading as quietly as possible down the stairs. My brain felt slow as I followed behind her. The cold of the old house seemed to sink into my skin, making my bones ache.

By the time I had squeaked and squawked my way downstairs, Lena had already wedged herself into the recliner with Alex. I couldn't even tell if he had woken up, or just instinctively wrapped his arms around her. It appeared the television had been forgotten; Lena suddenly seemed content to just shut her eyes and doze next to her boyfriend.

I sighed, but I couldn't make myself look away. There was something so intimate about the way they held each other, fiercely and delicately at the same time. I knew I was intruding, as I often was, but it comforted me to be a spectator to their peaceful moment.

When I finally pulled my eyes away from their sleeping forms, I looked for Raiden. He was already looking at me. He pulled himself upright on the couch for me to sit next to him. When he wrapped his arms around me I felt grounded, and less afraid of what laid outside these walls around us.

Raiden held me so gently against his chest, I had to keep looking back to make sure he was still there; and I wasn't just feeling warm air from where he had been before.

He met my eyes again and smiled. I had forgotten how much that simple gesture could warm my heart like I had a sun in my rib cage.

"I used to be so jealous of them," he confessed.

For a heartbeat, I was unsure of who he was talking about. I was unsure if there was even anyone on the planet besides us. Then his dark eyes flickered briefly to our sleeping friends and I understood.

"You aren't anymore?" I breathed into his shoulder.

I knew I often was, especially when things around us were as complicated as they were now. What Alex and Lena had always appeared so effortless.

"No," he said easily. "I was so self-centered that I could easily believe they had been put on this Earth just to further torture me as I paid for other people's sins. Ignoring how many of my own disasters I caused."

Raiden ran his fingers down the side of my neck, and I had to bite my tongue to keep from moaning.

"Now I have you, Marlow, and you are worth everything I have ever been through and so much more. You are worth everything."

When he bent down and kissed me it was like coming home from a very long day. It tasted of comfort and excitement, and a million other feelings at once. He tangled his hand through my long hair and I knew I'd gladly die again to feel like this forever.

FORTY-SEVEN

No matter how broken Lena gets, she can always pull together a convincing lie. Whether that was due to practice and their lifestyle, or her angelic face, I might never know.

But when my parents woke up, we were suddenly heading to Lena's for waffles and further parental supervision. I hoped one of those things were true. I was starving.

As it often is in the winter here, the sun never really rose that day. Gray skies stretched from one end of the world to the next like a lumpy comforter overhead, and thick new snow filled the roads, making the drive to the lake long and hazardous.

I wanted to keep my eyes closed, but the jarring made me carsick enough to change my mind. Skeletons don't get sick, I tried to tell myself. I still couldn't keep my eyes on the road as it was making us rock and slip and crawl along. So I kept my eyes on Raiden. He seemed so calm, like the kind of leader I knew he'd have to be someday, and like the kind of person I hoped I would grow into.

It amazed me how one minute he could seem like such a little boy with a broken heart, when in the next minute he was this man. In some ways, Raiden and I were so shockingly similar, but this radiation of strength was not something I could see in myself.

He asked me what I was thinking, even though I knew his eyes had ever left the road. He knew something was weighing heavily on my mind.

"It's just...we're so similar, like we really do share a soul."

"We do," he said evenly.

"Right," I agreed, "but we didn't always, and I was the same person... well, mostly," I added thinking of my recent self-improvements.

When at first he said nothing, I believed that I had said something completely detrimental to us, but he smiled, and that fear melted away like I wished the snow would.

"Marlow, if there was anything I have learned from my life in the last few years, it's that everything happens for a reason. I know now that we were always meant to be together. There is nothing in this world that I believe in more."

I wasn't sure if I had believed in destiny before that moment, that we could be born with some predetermined plan. Hearing Raiden talk about it filled something in me that I hadn't known was empty.

After driving for what felt like years, we arrived at the lake. The spot where the bones had been found on the road was staked with police tape, and there was a flapping tarp hung by wooden dowels that didn't manage to protect the crime scene from the new snow. One lone police car lay parked on the side of the road still, but the officer was asleep in the front seat as we drove past.

I tried to imagine what the lake must look like to outsiders as we pulled into the driveway no one else could see. It must have just been a barren field with a winter's worth of snow and ice. I couldn't make myself envision it.

"Raiden?" I asked. "You said yesterday, well, when you were talking about Conrad walking up to the barrier?"

"Yeah?" he said getting out of Melissa's Mercedes.

"So does that mean when you stay on the lakeside of the barrier that people can't see you? Not just the houses and the lake itself but *everything*?"

"Yes, but we're talking about magical borders. They are never going to be as steady and precise as lines on a map. Energy flows, and changes. Conrad could have easily been exposed."

We didn't go to Lena's house at all. Instead, we split into pairs in the open area between Lena and Raiden's, but we didn't go to his house either.

"Let's not go in yet," Raiden said leading me down the dock.

I went willingly, but I couldn't help but worry he was avoiding a confrontation that was going to have to happen regardless, and that seemed so unlike him. Biting my tongue selfishly I kept my suspicions to myself. I wanted this unspoiled moment together.

We rolled our pant legs up and stuck our feet in the warm lake. The blisters I had earned the night before healed immediately. I found myself mesmerized by the way I could see Raiden's blue glow through my own skin as he wrapped his foot around my ankle. I was so transfixed I didn't even hear the footsteps stomp up the dock behind us.

"Are you ever coming inside? Because— you do know our father don't you? He's about to blow a gasket in the most literal sense."

I turned around to watch Conrad shove his hands deep into his pockets, he looked like he would avoid going inside if he could, but I guessed Sara was still there waiting for him to come back. They had gotten so close, in even less time than Raiden and I had.

"I hadn't planned on it, actually," Raiden replied, but I elbowed him in the ribs.

"Fine," he said, "we're coming."

The scene inside was much the same as the day that Sara had come to stay at Skeleton Lake, only there were noticeably fewer people staring at us as we walked through the door. The kids at Iowa State hadn't come home, and I viewed that as a good sign. If we were facing some kind of war, here, now, I knew they would be sitting in this living room before me.

"Nice of you to finally join us," Abraham said curtly.

When I searched for sarcasm in his voice, there was none there. He looked exhausted, and I knew he was still furious with Raiden. However, his concern about the situation and the people of Skeleton Lake seemed to overpower his anger.

"The girl whose bones were found up the road..."

"Hana," Raiden added before I could. "Her name was Hana."

"Well," Abraham sighed, focusing his tired eyes on his adopted son for the first time that day, "someone dipped Hana into the lake."

I froze, terrified. The brief image I had seen of bones and shimmering pink fabric seared its way into my vision. That was what happened when normal people found themselves in Skeleton Lake. Even though people couldn't see the lake, it could kill them all the same. Even though the lake had powers to keep people away, those who knew it was there could still kill people with its power.

Remembering the way that lake water ate away at my clothes like acid, I realized what had happened to this girl's body at once. So had the others known all along?

"I don't suppose any of you know why she was targeted?" Abraham asked, but he didn't seem to have energy to hear the answer. "Not that it matters much, the poor girl's dead."

Then, like lightening, the truth was there in an electrifying flash.

I let out a shaky breath. I swore the weight of it would break my ribs. "They thought she was Lena."

Forty-Eight

"Excuse me?" Lena's father demanded.

"Well," I said, wondering if my reasoning would sound foolish outside my head, "she was blond, about the same size, and she was even wearing one of Lena's old dresses."

There were half a dozen other people in the room besides us, but everyone had gone still. Their minds were all busy working frantically to the same horrifying conclusion. It was just too big of a coincidence.

Raiden took my hand as Abraham spoke again, "Yes," he swallowed, "I thought it was something like that."

"Yeah," Raiden admitted, "me too. I have no idea what to do with that information. I've read all of the recorded history and never have we had to protect the lake from our own species."

I flinched at the word *species*. Another reminder that I was no longer human. I stared at Raiden in awe, and I wasn't the only one. Abraham was looking at his son like he hadn't seen him in years.

Raiden had been trying to come up with a solution on his own, and he hadn't said a word about it. I wanted to be furious with him, and on some level I was, but he looked so miserable it was hard to make those feelings stick. I knew he was only trying to spare me, he just needed to realize that part of the reason I existed was so he wouldn't have to bare this burden alone. He had to let me.

I squeezed his hand harder until he pulled away.

He ran his hand through his long, straw colored hair. "So what do we do? Do we wait here until they come looking for us? Do we try and find them first? Neither of those are good answers and both of them could end up getting us killed. I can't lose anyone else."

That was the problem. He would always worry someone would not make it through the next fight, and that knowledge was eating away at him.

I knew he felt responsible for Cassie's death. Given that the lake could heal almost anything, I assumed that meant they almost never lost a resident. They had all been children, spared from horrible ends, and they got to live the rest of their lives free of sickness and disease. They weren't used to death, not the kind that humans were used to.

No one had a good answer for Raiden, and Conrad wanted to find those responsible as fast as he could race out the door. His willingness to risk his neck only made Sara sob from the bit of floor space she had been perched on.

We still weren't sure, but it was looking more and more likely that Christian—Lance's dad—was the one responsible for Hana's death.

Raiden assured me that there were other beasts, terrible beasts that roamed the night and preyed on women. While that wasn't at all comforting, at least I knew it could be something else, maybe something easier to get rid of. Only the likelihood of something showing up now was slim, and no monster with teeth and claws would explain the pristine pink dress. Besides, Abraham had seemed positive the lake had killed her, and real Skeleton's wouldn't have been able to walk back to the road if it had really been an accident.

Slowly, people trickled back to their own houses. No one felt any better at our lack of solutions. I had quickly become too preoccupied with all the paranormal creatures that could kill you to be any help, and I was starting to feel like I never again wanted to leave the lake—only it wasn't safe here anymore either.

My skin felt like cement, squeezing me much too tight. My stomach felt like my heart had lodged itself there. The pain was frightening and never ending.

After everyone—even Abraham—had wandered away, Sara called her mom. She hadn't wanted to risk it before when she had been worried Christian would come looking for her; but now we were almost positive he was already here. Our suspicions were confirmed less than thirty seconds into the phone call.

The other Hollows had made it back to The Dead Sea. They had little money and the trip back was long and hard. Then they replayed what had happened at Skeleton Lake. As expected, Christian hadn't been too terribly disturbed about his son's death—he had been furious that two females had managed to get away.

Sara's mom said that Christian had launched an official crusade against us, and I chuckled under my breath about the historical reference. She continued to tell us what that entailed and I abruptly stopped laughing.

Christian had come this time in an effort to convert us. He wanted us to conform to his lifestyle, which as far as I could tell was ruthless. It also seemed to revolve around creating more Hollows, which for the most part, the residents of Skeleton Lake seemed to be against.

So we all knew how that was going to go.

"The funny thing is," Sara said after promising her mother she'd be careful, "is that Christian's whole goal used to be making Hollows equal to everyone else. Skeleton Lake is as close to that as anywhere else, only that won't be enough anymore. He doesn't care how many he has to kill. He won't stop until he has *you*."

I felt Raiden tense next to me. "We won't let that happen," he said.

"I know," Sara said sadly. "I also know he's counting on that."

"So how do we find him?" Conrad asked her quietly, but Sara just shrugged.

"You won't have to worry about that. He will find you."

FORTY-NINE

It was just before dinner when my parents sent me a text to remind me they had bingo night at church. I saw my window of opportunity to get clothes from home without an audience. I decided to take it.

Raiden couldn't take me, though, and I understood. He had to sit down with Conrad and Sara for a talk, hoping to discover something about Christian that would help us. So far we had nothing, but he wouldn't hear of letting me go by myself, so he asked Alex to take me.

Several people had popped in and out today to check on our progress. They wanted a plan. It was unnerving how the adults of Skeleton Lake seemed to look toward a group of children to save their whole existence. Even Abraham hadn't bothered to reappear before Alex had come to get me.

We walked to the garage by his house, but instead of getting in his shiny red sports car, he directed me to a large blue SUV.

"It's my mom's, and it smells like lavender, but it does have all-wheel drive."

"Lena's not coming with us?" I asked before climbing into the passenger seat.

"Nah. I mean, no offense, but it's easier for me if I only have to protect one of you."

"Sorry," I mumbled. He shrugged it off and climbed into the driver's seat. I wondered if it really was too dangerous for me to leave, and I realized Raiden would have thrown a fit if he hadn't wanted me to go.

"It's not your fault, Marlow, and I doubt anything will happen—I just want to be careful."

Last time he drove me anywhere he had ended up in a fight on the side of the road with Lance.

As it turned out, the Land Rover handled

the snow great. I sank into the heated leather seat as we started down County Road Nine. Then we met our first problem.

The squad car that had been parked by the ditch was blocking the whole road. Lights were flashing violently in the new night sky.

"Now, what the hell?" Alex asked, slowing down.

As we got closer we saw exactly what the hell. The police officer was slumped into his seat, almost exactly how he had been when we passed by him before. Only this time, it was obvious he was dead, and not just asleep.

Thick drops of blood had dripped down his neck from where his throat had been slashed from one ear to the other. The wound was jagged and torn. Not a knife wound for sure.

"Oh my God," Alex said before throwing the Land Rover into park.

He flung himself out of the door and tore down the snowy way. In hindsight, that had been a horrible mistake. We should have turned around and gone back to the lake, but Alex wouldn't leave until he knew he couldn't help this man—I knew by his eyes it was too late.

Alex ripped his glove off and held his naked wrist against the man's mouth, and then he shook his head. I supposed that meant he had confirmed the man was no longer breathing. He had just turned around to walk back when the skeleton walked out of the ditch where he'd been hiding.

I knew at once it was Christian. He looked like Lance—they even had the same colored hair and vile smirk. But he was wearing drawstring linen pants, and a short sleeve shirt, and his feet were completely bare. Three fingers on each horrible hand were nothing but bones, and exposed collarbones peeked out of the shirt he hadn't bothered to button.

I screamed just in time for Alex to jerk around before Christian grabbed him. The Hollow, with his bone fingers, slashed at Alex's jacket just above the elbows. I watched as my friend tried to land a punch, but Christian got his hands around Alex's neck first.

Crimson ran from three large gashes on either side if Alex's neck, but the monster did not let go. So Alex kicked him in the shin with one of his black boots and that just made Christian toss him into the ditch like he was a rag doll before stalking after him.

Alex didn't move from where he landed. I swallowed down another scream and crept out the door of the SUV.

Christian was laughing when he reached Alex but I couldn't run. He'd hear me if I did. Grabbing Alex by the shoulders, he sank his ghastly fingers deep into the muscle.

Alex screamed, but not a normal scream —it reminded me of the eerie song that sprung from my throat when I was in trouble. It would completely block out what I was about to do.

Christian was still tangled up with Alex, who had gone completely limp in the snow. The wailing and laughter permeated the stillness of winter. No one heard me pull a thick wooden dowel up from the police scene, and no one heard me plunge it through Christian's chest.

The sound it made shattered everything else. I knew it didn't sound like it should, though I had nothing to go by. The dowel slid right through Christian and into the frozen ground. I was surprised at my own strength, but Christian never stopped laughing. He had been pinned to the ground, but it wouldn't last.

My eyes avoided the gore that covered the top of Alex's body as I dragged his limp form out of the ditch. I instead focused on his face, which was too pale and smeared with blood. If he died, it would be my fault.

I managed to drag him all the way back to the Land Rover and pushed him into the backseat. As I slid into the driver's seat, I chanced a look to where I had left Christian, just in time to watch him pull the stick from his chest and throw it back into the ditch. In the white beneath him there were two bloody snow angels.

I threw the SUV into reverse.

FIFTY

I laid on the horn before the house even came into view. Conrad and Raiden had already begun sprinting the distance to Lena's before I pulled into her drive.

Laurel ripped open the front door, when she saw who was driving she started to scream. Lena was only steps behind her.

I raced to open the back door, drenched in blood. I had just jerked the door open when the boys ran up behind me. Conrad got to us first, but neither of them had time for questions. Conrad took one look at Alex and roughly slid him out of the backseat. To my horror, the boy did not make a sound.

Conrad threw Alex over one shoulder and ran back toward the lake. I saw him give his brother a frantic, pained expression as Raiden caught up to them.

It felt as though all the blood was running out of my body even though I was merely a spectator to this disaster. Lena was right on the boy's heels. I swore when I looked at Raiden he was crying, and that was when I broke.

Laurel was staring at me, I waited for her to scream and blame me, but she only took me into her arms and let me cry.

The scene was all too familiar, only this time it wasn't Conrad close to death, but Alex. The only similarities were that both times it was entirely my fault.

Someone else was screaming, and I looked over Laurel's shoulder to see Alex's mom run into the lake after her son.

"He'll be okay," Raiden said, so loudly I knew it was for my benefit. Everyone else had gathered on the end of the closest dock, watching the spectacle in the water.

"Marlow," Laurel whispered, and I pulled my head up to look at her face, only she was looking behind me. Instinctively I knew what was there. "Marlow," she said again, "you have to run."

So I ran, and Laurel screamed so I didn't have to. It didn't seem to matter though, because Christian didn't appear to be in a hurry to catch up to us. Then we were on the dock with everyone else.

"I know what you're thinking," Lena's father said calmly, "but we seriously outnumber you."

Christian laughed, and it was nothing like it was before. This time it was quick and bitter.

"I know what you're thinking," Christian mocked them, "but you're an idiot. Hello Sara, funny running into you here."

"Go to hell, Christian!" she screamed from the front of the dock.

"I already lived it, sweet lips."

I watched as Sara recoiled. Christian was way too foul to hit on anyone. Lance had been bad enough.

"You aren't playing by your usual rules," Sara spat, but she was walking further down the dock to the rest of the group.

"Aww, you noticed. Too bad you didn't notice what a group of losers you decided to align yourself with. But I'll cut you a deal—you agree to come back to me right now, and I promise not to hurt you."

"You're lying," she said simply, "and I wouldn't go with you even if you weren't."

"Oh, you caught me," Christian said placing his grotesque hands on his blood stained hips. "I'm going to kill you either way. At least now I can tell your poor, sweet mother that I gave you a chance without having to have a guilty conscious."

Everything out of Christian's mouth was so ludicrous that it would have all been completely laughable, if he hadn't looked so terrifying. Raiden trudged out of the lake. His brilliant blue bones shone like normal, only his eyes were more intense.

"This is your only warning!" he shouted, making a straight line to Christian. "Leave here now, or die here *now*. Those are your only choices."

Christian eyed Raiden skeptically, trying to figure out if he was any type of threat.

"And you must be the Champion," he said when he was done.

But I didn't know what he meant by that.

"That's right," Raiden said. "And I am ordering you away from Skeleton Lake."

With that, Christian's horrid laughter returned full force.

"I guess we'll see about that, kid," Christian chuckled. I did notice that he took a step back away from Raiden.

"I killed Lance, you know," Raiden said indifferently. "And I can kill you too. I think you know that, don't you?"

I wanted to scream at him to shut up, but I couldn't open my mouth for fear that every sob I had kept inside would come out. Raiden hadn't seen what Christian was like; we did not want to see him angrier.

"I wondered," Christian said flatly. "A regrettable thing, to be sure, but it's not like I can't make more."

I nearly retched, and when I looked back up from my feet I noticed Abraham inching his way down the dock as Raiden kept Christian's attention. As soon as the man's feet hit the grass he was running, but I think Christian knew what he was up to all along.

Just as Abraham was within striking distance, Christian turned to reach out with both bare arms and snap the old man's neck.

The crack echoed all around the lake, and then thunder began to crash overhead. A storm was forming around us, and Melissa was singing.

"The skeleton song," Laurel whispered, "The song your soul sings when it needs its other half. This is the last time she will ever sing it. She will sing until her throat is red and raw, and she will never sing it again."

Laurel was crying. "I never had him. Not really. It was always her."

Abraham was dead and Christian thought that was hilarious. He was the only one. In his anger, Raiden marched right up to the Hollow. Alex had come, too, and was weakly clinging to Conrad in an effort to keep him from flying after them.

Christian tried to swat Raiden away, but Raiden was quicker. Faster than I knew he could move.

"You think you can end me so easily boy?

I am the first guardian of treachery—and you haven't even realized you're in hell yet."

Something snapped inside me. Quick and cutting as a whip. Hell felt more real in that second than it ever had in a church pew.

Despite his words, Christian defensively. He walked inches back when there were so few inches left to give.

His motions were jerky, too harsh looking to be human. He avoided Raiden's fist with a swooping, courtly bow—but he never stood back up.

Raiden thrust one blue hand behind Christian's exposed breastbone and ripped out his heart.

A fitting end to a beast I swore didn't have one. A quick demise to begin a memory that would haunt me for the rest of my life.

THE END

Later that night, I called my parents to tell them that Raiden's father had died. I didn't need any other excuses to keep me at the lake after that. Anyway, it was going to be a short stay. In the next few days, Raiden was leaving to take Sara back to The Dead Sea, and I was going with him.

There were things he said he needed to take care of, and he didn't know when he would be back, but I couldn't stay behind. He didn't even after seeing what had happened to his parents. He wanted me with him as much as I wanted him with me.

Just as Laurel had said, Melissa sang until

she was silent, and then the tears came like they would never stop. She had spent so many years being angry with him, that I thought the regret might kill her too.

Rain poured down from the sky above the lake, and I stared up at it as it pelted my face with fat raindrops like warm tears. Lena said the lake was crying, and that it had done it before when Cassie had died. Was the lake really alive? Did it share our pain?

Conrad said he, too, would be going to The Dead Sea with Sara, claiming there was nothing to keep him here any longer. Raiden disagreed. I couldn't help but wonder if our trip involved trying to talk him into coming home. Either way, it would be an adventure, but most of all, it was a distraction.

I wish I could do more to help Raiden, but if there was one thing I had learned since coming to the lake, it's that skeletons do regret—and there is nothing to be done about it.

About the Author

Find Author Angela Kulig all over the
internet:
www.angelakulig.com
www.facebook.com/authorangelakulig
www.twitter.com/angelakulig
www.instagram.com/authorangelakulig

Hollows Series Books:
The Skeleton Song
Skeleton Lake
Dead Sea
The Desert of Ash- COMING SOON
Bone Deep (a Skeleton Lake Novella)-
COMING SOON
Ice Bridge Forest-COMING SOON

Other Books:
The Wayward and the Wicked Series
Docia Departed

Docia Incarnate
Fox Fallen

for more visit angelakulig.com

THE SKELETON SONG

The water was darker than the starless sky above, and far more ominous. I gazed at it, like I hoped to see the heavens lurking there instead of blackness. But that night, God was nowhere to be found.

I didn't even know if He existed, and I had heard hundreds of sermons in my short life. There was only a bloodless lump behind my heart where that kind of love should have been, and in another three steps I would be just as dead to him as he was to me.

I was only three years old, but I could swim. It was far too cold for that sort of thing, so my nose was numb, and so were my fingers. I hadn't wanted to go into that murky, bottomless lake, where I knew that I'd swim forever, or be killed. Or maybe both.

The whole thing seemed to hum, like the electric fence in my first family's yard. Thinking of my parents made something stir behind that immovable lump, but I doubted I had ever loved them, even at such a young age. I had already been told I would never see them again. I can't remember if that hurt, but I don't think it did.

So I glanced back at my new family instead. I didn't love them either. Nor did they love me. If they had, they would have never made me go in that water. They wouldn't have had that man walk toward me like he'd take me away from the fear, only to throw me into the abyss and into the belly of the beast.

They would have let the disease take me. That's what love would have gotten me--an easier death.

The splash came before I was ready. Like the prick of a needle to draw blood on every inch of my skin. No one jumped in to save me, so I burned. First, the little eyelet dress that I had arrived in. The water swished below my arms and feet, but it seared like a fire.

After the dress went my skin. The water smelled like burning hair and it made me gag between wails. I knew I should be dead, but somehow, I could still hear my screams. They went on and on, long after I could no longer tell I was smoldering.

Finally, it was over.

Strong arms took me from the water and sat me down on the dock. That short moment of flight was the best feeling of my entire existence. Only the arms weren't arms at all, they were nothing but green bones in bags that were the shape of limbs. The appearance of the man should have shocked me, but my own body was far worse.

I had expected there to be blisters and blood, but there was nothing there but x-ray like bones and the same transparent skin.

Though drowning isn't the way that most adventures start, it is the only way at Skeleton Lake.

"I'm glad I can't remember it," Raiden says. It's a lie just for me. We are alone with the smell of weathered wood and the summertime.

I've known he was lying for years. Drowning isn't something you forget. Even if eventually the lake and the memory stopped eating away at you, it stayed inside your bones.

I had known better than to bring it up though, so I let him change the subject with a kiss. Mouths were better used than this, bringing up painful memories, and Raiden tasted like taffy and the best kind of daydreams.

His hands wandered, learning my body with skin and clothes, counting my ribs though he could see them whenever he wanted. Tugging on my waist until the space between us was nothing but a memory. His hair caught the light like it was made of it, and his arms were warmer and more addicting.

Raiden was smiling when he leaned in to kiss me again, and I was ashamed to admit I hadn't realized I had stopped. An errant thought had sprung to mind and refused to release me, like thorns that had dug into my flesh.

I couldn't believe the boy that I was once too afraid to touch was kissing me a third time, tasting me like I was always at the tip of his tongue.

We were thirteen, and it would have been easy to say I had always loved him. It was also untrue. Through most of our childhood, Raiden Mast had been a bit of an ass. Sometimes, he still was, but it was easy to forget on days like this. On days where it seemed like our whole life would be filled with clear skies and endless summers. When pain was nothing but a distant memory.

The whole reason I was at Skeleton Lake was to be with my soul mate and Raiden was mine, but if Raiden Mast was a bit of an ass, Conrad Mast was seated firmly in the dictionary next to complete douche-bag. And that was the least of his faults.

The day I found out who I had been left on this Earth for, Conrad took it worse than anyone else. Even me, and I had a fantastic meltdown.

Though with time I grew into the idea, there were moments when I still didn't know why. Those were the days that Conrad found me. Days where I was alone, even if it was by choice. He liked to think we had that in common.

On those days Conrad would pull me close, and kiss me like he had no right to do. He couldn't even unclench his teeth, but I knew what he meant.

Pre-Order Now

www.ingramcontent.com/pod-product-compliance
Lightning Source LLC
Chambersburg PA
CBHW061859310726
48972CB00004B/1088